Foreword

Other books by Terry Cubbins:

Smuggler's Blues, a memoir

There'll Come a Time

The Stringer

for more info and to view trailer for *The Stringer,* see:

TerryCubbins.com

Life in the Left Hand Lane

The Glory Daze of 'Maverick' Jim Swanson

by

Terry Cubbins

Introduction

The first time I met Jim Swanson he was working as a greeter/security guy at the entrance to Suncadia, a resort with high-end golf courses and luxury homes, near Roslyn, Washington. I was on my way to hit golf balls at the resort's driving range, a facility I had been to a hundred times before.

I was motoring along, well below the posted speed limit of 19 mph, when a man wearing a greeter's uniform came bouncing out of the kiosk and yelling at me. He reminded me a little of Robert De Niro.

"Hey! Wait a minute! Where you goin'?" He asked.

I figured he was a new employee who was taking his job much too seriously. I was a little annoyed but I stopped right where I was. He caught up to my car, placed both hands on the windowsill, leaned in and said, "So, you wanna talk to me or somethin'?"

It caught me by surprise, and my knee-jerk reaction was to laugh. "Why would I want to do that? Who are you?"

"I'm Jim Swanson" he said smiling. "People call me Swannie." He looked at me as if that answered my question.

It didn't, so I asked, "Swannie? After the river?"

"River?"

Obviously, we weren't connecting, and then it dawned on me what was going on. I work for a radio station in the area and was driving my SUV with the station's logo on it. Sometimes strangers will chat me up or comment about something they heard on the radio. Lots of folks with suggestions about the format or playlist.

By now a couple of cars had backed up behind me, but the man called Swannie just stood up and waved them around. Unfortunately, going around meant the passing vehicles would

1

have to veer off the pavement a little, just enough to flatten a few wildflowers before getting back on the road, wild flowers that the resort probably spent a considerable sum on when they landscaped the place. Nevertheless, Swannie seemed unconcerned with the situation, like it was collateral damage or something, and got back in my face again.

"So... you think you might wanna interview me? Everybody else does."

"…Uhm, not to seem impolite, but I still don't know you, or why I would want to, interview you, that is."

"Okay, stay here, I'll be right back." He dodged traffic and ran back into his duty station.

I started to pull off to the side of the road, but now cars were going around me on both sides, so I stayed where I was and turned on my flashers. My new friend soon stepped back out of the kiosk, held up his hand for all traffic to stop, and then trotted back to my car with a copy of the *Seattle Times* newspaper in his hand. "Here, look at this." While I opened the paper, he went back to directing traffic around me.

On the front page was a group picture of the 1975 Portland Mavericks' Single-A baseball team. The accompanying story was written by Larry Stone and titled, *"The Nuttiest Team in Baseball."*

Swanson leaned back in my window and pointed to a player in the photo. "There, that's me. The one in the middle. The only left-handed catcher in baseball. The guy next to me is Kurt Russell, you know, the actor? The fellow next to him is Jim Bouton. Good guy. Great pitcher too. He was making a comeback. I caught him all the time."

He stopped long enough to wave more traffic around us and then leaned back into the window.

"They made a documentary about the Mavericks too. It's called, *The Battered Bastards of Baseball.* It's on Netflix."

He delivered all of this information so quickly that I struggled to listen fast enough. I'm old enough to remember Jim Bouton when he pitched for the Yankees in a couple of World Series games. He had a really good fast ball then and threw with such ferocity that his cap would fly off after every pitch. Later, after a short stint with the Seattle Pilots. He wrote *Ball Four*, a behind-the-scenes expose about some of the drug use and partying that went on after, and during, games. He was gallant enough to include himself among those who indulged in the shenanigans. And, I knew Kurt Russell had been a good athlete and at one time had a promising career in baseball. Still, I was naturally skeptical, but a documentary on Netflix? Easy enough to prove. Picture on the *Seattle Times* front page? Right in front of me. Left-handed catcher? Hmm...

"I also opened the first comedy-club in the Northwest in '82," said the man in my window. "Downtown Seattle. Called Swannies. The first comedian to play my place was Jerry Seinfeld. You've heard of him, right?"

I smiled and said I had heard of him.

"Cheech and Chong, Ellen DeGeneres. All those guys played my place."

Now he really had my attention. I pulled off the road and flattened a few wildflowers myself. I wanted to hear more from this man called Swannie.

CHAPTER ONE

Of all the people on Earth, only one in ten are left-handed. You may have heard of a few of them: Albert Einstein, Leonardo da Vinci, Mozart, Beethoven, Mark Twain, Neil Armstrong, Babe Ruth, Jim Swanson.

Okay, maybe not Jim Swanson so much, but then again, I hadn't heard of him either. Not until he told me he was the only left-handed person to sign a professional baseball contract to play catcher as his primary position.

Of course, there have been a few left-handed professional baseball players that sat behind the plate for an inning or two but catching was not their first position. And, most of those lefties who *did* catch, played in the late 1800's when the term 'southpaw' was coined for left-handed pitchers. The name 'southpaw' came about when baseball diamonds were designed so the batter would face east to avoid looking into an afternoon sun. A left-handed pitcher's hand, or paw, would appear to the batter as if it were coming out of the south. Apparently, nobody thought it necessary to call a right-handed pitcher a 'northpaw'.

Why no left-handed catchers in baseball? There are several theories. The early notion was that since most batters were right-handed at the time, and stood on the *left* side of the plate, a left-handed catcher would bonk the batter in the back of the head when throwing to second, or third base for that matter.

This theory was actually endorsed by Branch Rickey, *thee* Branch Rickey, who played such a huge part in baseball from the early1900's until his death in 1965. He was elected to Baseball's Hall of Fame as an executive in 1967. Rickey was a noble man probably best known for signing Jackie Robinson to a contract with the Brooklyn Dodgers, thus integrating Major League Baseball. Rickey was around baseball all of his life, even making it to 'the show' briefly as a player. (He batted left-handed but caught right-handed.) With that much credibility you should have some respect for his opinion, right? Well, one afternoon while

Rickey was having his cup of coffee in the 'bigs', he caught a game and set a record that still stands today: the opposing team stole 13 bases on him. He was a good sport about it though and after the game he was quoted as saying, "They ran so much on me I thought my arm was gonna fall off."

Of course, by then, maybe there were a lot of more *left-handed batters* in the league, so maybe Rickey hit a few of those batters in the back of the head while trying to throw to second?

(He also holds the record for people I know who went by the name of "Branch.")

Another theory has it that if a left-hander throws to second from home plate, there's a natural propensity for the ball to tail away toward the shortstop side of second base, away from the runner. Right-handed throws are just the opposite.

Still another hypothesis dealt with plays at the plate. If a throw came in from the outfield, especially from center or right, a lefty catcher would have to first catch the ball in his gloved right hand and then swing it back toward a runner who is most likely rolling in hard from outside of the third-base foul line.

The above-mentioned theory seems to be the most popular, but if you ask our boy, Jim Swanson, aka Swannie, he'll tell you that *all* those theories are bullshit. "I really don't understand why people say you can't be a catcher if you're left-handed. It's not a big deal. Just position your feet for whatever the situation calls for, and you'll be fine."

CHAPTER TWO

When Jim Swanson was born on January 10, 1953, in Portland, Oregon, he didn't just pop out and decide to be left-handed; he grew into it as most lefties do.

However, if he had known the challenges ahead, he might have made an effort to go righty. Scissors, power saws, doorknobs, sporting equipment, saluting, writing, these are just a few things that can put a lefty out of his or her comfort zone.

Even some languages tend to discriminate against lefties. In English, to do something 'right' is to do something correctly. One Latin word for 'right' is 'sane.' The Italian word for *left,* 'sinistra' comes from the Latin word for sinister. In some Spanish countries, to do something 'por izquierda', or to the left, is synonymous with doing something shady. The Boston Strangler, Jack-the-Ripper, John Dillinger, Billy the Kid, and O.J. Simpson all swung from the left. So, there you go.

Of course, lefties do have *some* advantages over righties, they're better overall in fistfights, (apparently there's a surprise factor involved) *and* they can see better underwater!

So, I guess the point here is; be extra vigilant if you get in an argument with a left-handed person, especially if you're both underwater at the time.

CHAPTER THREE

Growing up in Vancouver, Washington, little Jimmy didn't see any problems with being left-handed. He pulled girls' pigtails and threw rocks through windows with the best of them. He had a good arm even then.

His parents thought that a Catholic up-bringing might serve him well as a moral compass, so they enrolled him in Our Lady of The Lourdes Elementary School where he spent grades one through eight. No doubt his folks were proud of him when he was selected as an altar boy at the age of ten.

The jury is still out on how the moral teachings part went at Our Lady, but Jimmy, who we'll now refer to as Swannie, did pick up some business acumen when he learned that he could make five dollars every time someone needed an altar boy for a wedding or a funeral. Swannie augmented those earnings with a daily paper route where he perfected a quick, snappy delivery, mostly on target to doorsteps. He experimented with a few tosses right-handed, but the newspapers tended to sail on him, and sometimes flapped open. In the end, he stuck with his left hand. He could really bring it from the left.

During his formative years at Our Lady of the Lourdes, Swannie would sometimes stray from the straight and narrow. Like the time he asked one of the nuns for a date. Out of habit I suppose.

Antics like those drew the attention of Father O'Brien who ran the show at the Lourdes with a heavy hand and a sense of the dramatic. The school building that he lorded over was built in a horseshoe shape with a courtyard in the middle. All classrooms faced inward toward this courtyard. When a student got in trouble, such as young Swannie, Father O'Brien would personally administer punishment in the middle of this courtyard. Father O'Brien's preferred method of social control was spanking. And not to miss a great teaching moment, he would order all classes to be let out momentarily to witness said punishment.

These teaching moments might help explain why Swannie adapted to a catcher's position so easily, or why he is still a natural at mooning people.

On the playground, and during organized athletics, Swannie excelled. He loved sports and played them all well. During baseball season, his favorite position was catching because that's where the action was. He was in on every pitch. No lollygagging around in the outfield for him, no siree. Tossing a glove in the air just to stay busy? Not for Swannie. Nobody to talk to in the outfield? *Bor-ring*. Although he would later earn a college scholarship to play center field, his first love was catching.

Swannie learned to talk at an early age and hasn't stopped since. At home plate he had people to chat up, batters, umpires, pitchers, dugout personnel, essentially anybody within chatting distance. And if he wanted to play the part of field general and talk to the whole team, Swannie could do that too. "Alright you guys, be awake out there," he'd say. "Let's go. Little chatter now. Hum, baby."

Or to the opposing batter; "Nice swing, Alice."

Of course, as a kid, Swannie's first challenge was just *finding* a left-handed catcher's mitt. When he couldn't locate one, he borrowed a right-handed glove, flipped it around, and learned to catch that way.

(photo: Sue Swanson)

Lady of Lourdes; Swannie as a promising Altar Boy, front row, just left of center

(photo: Sue Swanson)

Little League team: Swannie front row, 3rd from left. Swannie would later borrow $5000 from Coach Berke, far right, to open his sports bar.

Swannie's father, Earle Swanson, was a great supporter of his son and always offered encouragement in whatever sport or position he wanted to play. Earle Swanson admired his son's courage and, even though money was tight at the time, he paid to have a left-handed catcher's mitt custom made for his son.

Although he would never talk about it, Earle Swanson knew a thing or two about courage himself. In Europe during World War 11, Swanson piloted B-25's on 66 bombing missions. On mission number 38, his plane was hit by enemy fire that ruptured his fuel tanks. He was able to maneuver the plane over to the Mediterranean Sea just before it ran out of fuel. He made a perfect 'dead-stick' water landing enabling him and his entire crew to make it into life rafts before the aircraft sank. Swanson and his crew were rescued two hours later by a passing Italian supply ship.

Swanson received the Distinguished Flying Medal for saving himself and his crew.

Before Swanson was through, he would also earn the Air Medal with 8 Oak Leaf Clusters, Distinguished Unit Citation, EAME Theater Ribbon, Purple Heart Medal, and 5 Battle Stars in different campaigns.

Swanson's total of 66 missions is a staggering amount of bombing runs. There might have even been more, maybe just one more, if it hadn't of been for one thing: after landing number 66, Earle Swanson wasn't able to move from the cockpit. His crew had to pry him loose from the controls. He wasn't sick or wounded physically, but he was done. Like an internal circuit breaker had tripped saying, "Sorry, pal, that's it. You can't do this anymore. You'll fry what's left of your soul if you even try."

In the 1949 movie, *"Twelve O'clock High,"* Gregory Peck played the part of an Army Air Wing Commander flying missions during WW 11. He is a tireless commander who pushes himself and his men to the limit in an effort to save the world from Nazism. In one of the last scenes of the movie, Peck is on the tarmac getting ready to lead his squadron on another mission. As he begins to pull himself into the belly of his bomber, his synapses suddenly pop, and he's toast. He became mentally and physically paralyzed and had to be led away from his aircraft.

In an 'art imitating life' scenario, Peck's character could have easily been modeled after Earle Swanson.

Coincidentally, one of Earle Swanson's co-pilots during the war was Jack Valenti who flew 51 missions himself. After serving in the military, Valenti became a political consultant and was in President Kennedy's motorcade on that fateful day in Dallas.

Valenti was also on Air Force One as it flew back to Washington immediately after the assassination. In the famous photo of LBJ, right hand raised, taking the oath of president, Jack Valenti is seated left of LBJ and Jackie Kennedy, who was still dressed in her blood-stained pink suit and pill box hat. Jack Valenti later went on to become president of The Motion Picture Academy in Hollywood.

Because Earle Swanson didn't like to talk about the war and his part in it, Jim Swanson only found out about some of these things as research developed for this book.

"My dad was a quiet man and didn't do a lot of talking in general," Swannie said. "He was especially tight-lipped about the war and his part in it. But my mom did say after the war he confided in her on a few things that bothered him, like the time he was ordered to bomb an orphanage in Germany. I'm guessing that the Nazis were using the orphanage to stash something evil there, but I don't know if my dad ever found out for sure what was what, he just did his job."

Swannie also reflected, "My dad was a hero to a lot of people, but none more so than me. I know he didn't like to talk much about himself or the war, maybe that's why I talk so much now. You know, making up for my dad?"

If Earle Swanson was alive today, he might feel uncomfortable with someone writing about him in a book that's about his son. Sorry, Mr. Swanson, but you sir, deserve remembrance. Thank you for your service.

(photo: Fold3)

Captain Earle Swanson

(photo: Fold3)

Captain Swanson's B-25, "Twin Engine Sadie"

CHAPTER FOUR

In 1969, Swannie began high school at Fort Vancouver High, in Vancouver, Washington. He was 15 years old, 5' 9", and weighed in at 135. Not that big a kid, but he was getting to the point where he was too big to paddle, by teachers or anybody else.

Physique-wise you could say Swannie was wiry with a personality to match. He was brash, funny, and scrappy, but most of all, he was loyal. If he liked you, he had your back. He was the kind of guy you wanted on your side. He kept his brown hair at modest length and his shoes shined.

As a freshman, Swannie made the varsity baseball team as a catcher and center fielder. And even though he still had the attention span of a puppy, he somehow managed to stay out of trouble. In his sophomore year he got his first car, a red Volkswagen Beetle, and his first real girlfriend, a brunette. Even with these distractions, Swannie kept his grade point average up to a respectable level.

However, it was soon evident it wasn't his grade point average that was getting people's attention; it was his batting average. Perhaps the paddling that Father O'Brien dished out had made a difference. Instead of taking a pounding on his butt, Swannie started doing some pounding of his own, on baseballs. Better to give than receive, no?

Although he wasn't considered a home run hitter, Swannie stung the ball and sprayed it to all fields. In his junior year, he led the league in doubles and triples and batted .439. Swannie was also throwing out runners from behind the plate as well as from center field and was selected to the All-City team.

Swannie's senior year was more of the same. He made only one error all season and finished his high school career with a .452 batting average.

Of course, by this time there were college recruiters and scouts looking at him. He was offered several scholarships from schools in the Northwest, but eventually chose to stay close to home and girlfriend, attending Clark Jr College and paying his own way.

CHAPTER FIVE

For his first two years in junior college, Swannie played baseball for the Clark 'Penguins' and continued to excel in all categories of the game. His bat stayed hot even as his romance cooled. And then at the end of his tenure at Clark, one of the recruiters that had been following his career came calling again. His name was Gary Frederick, and he was representing Central Washington University, located in Ellensburg, Washington.

Mr. Frederick was, and is, an honest, hard-working man who started his head-coaching career for the CWU Wildcats in 1968 when he was just twenty-nine years old. Due in large part to the war in Vietnam, the average age of the players on Coach Frederick's first team, was twenty-four years old, a lot of them veterans of the war.

Frederick loved the fact that his players came in all shapes, sizes, colors, and personalities, and the military guys already knew how to play as a team. *Wild*cats? You bet.

Thus, the tone of the players that Frederick looked for had been set early on and Swannie fit that bill perfectly.

We mentioned Gary Frederick is an honest man, but it almost cost him when he first approached Swannie. Swannie liked Frederick from the get-go, but hesitated to sign with him when Frederick told him, "If you come to Central, the thing you're *not* going to do is catch! You're too good a hitter, fielder, *and* you can run fast! Besides, all that crap a catcher's gotta wear; chest protector, shin guards, face mask, they're called 'tools of ignorance' for a reason, son."

This didn't make Frederick a bad guy, far from it, he just already had a catcher that could throw a baseball so hard it made hissing sounds.

In fact, Gary Frederick's integrity was unquestionable. It was one of the reasons in his tenure at Central he was able to wear so many different hats, including Athletic Director, before retiring in 2010.

But it was while Frederick was serving as coach of the women's fast-pitch softball team in 2008 that his sense of integrity really reared its lovely head. In a vital home game against rival Western Oregon, with the score tied and two runners on, Oregon outfielder, Sara Tucholsky came to the plate. Sara, who had never hit a home run in her life, not even in her dreams, knocked it out of the park. Sara of course was not familiar in the art of a home trot. She began her journey by promptly cutting in front of first base without touching the bag. Realizing her error, she stopped quickly, too quickly as it turned out, and she felt something tear in her leg. She was able to gimp back to the bag, but that's as far as she could go.

Oregon coaches and players immediately huddled with the umpires to see what their options were. The rules stated that her team cannot help her, other than bringing in a pinch runner who must remain at first base with Sara being credited for a single.

That's when two Washington infielders, Liz Wallace and Mallory Holtman, took matters into their own hands, literally. Learning that there was no rule against the *defense* helping Sara, they picked her up and carried her around the bases, lowering her down at each base, letting her touch the bag with her good foot.

When interviewed after the game, the two Central players gave credit to their coach for the inspiration for what they did. "We just reflect what Coach Frederick instills in all of his programs."

Oregon went on to win the game 4-2 and later won the Conference Championship. The incident would later be talked about on the all sport shows throughout the country. ESPN awarded it an 'ESPY' (Excellence in Sports Performance Yearly Award) for one of the best sports moments of the year. Long time radio and television commentator Paul Harvey highlighted it on his news program as well.

CHAPTER SIX

In his first season playing center field for Central, Swannie soon found out that Frederick could metaphorically play hardball, too. Such an occasion arose in a game when Swannie was at the plate and took a called third strike ending the inning. Not agreeing with the umpire, Swannie put up an argument. Frederick came out of the dugout to protect his player and after the dust settled, had a word with the young man. All went well until Swannie's next at bat when he found himself in the same situation, again called out on strikes, and again putting up a stink.

This time Frederick did nothing and let Swannie rant and rave while the umpire calmly walked away. When the two teams exchanged places in the field, Frederick still said nothing. It wasn't until Swannie had taken his position in center field and everyone was set to resume play that Frederick stepped out of the dugout and called a time-out.

Then Frederick made a big production of trotting out a substitute player to inform Swannie that he was being relieved of his duties for the day.

Frederick liked his team's energy but at times had to apply discipline to keep the vigor flowing in the right direction. Once during practice there was a dust up between a couple of players near a batting cage. Frederick didn't see who had instigated it but when he got near the scene, he saw Swannie and immediately shoved him up against the cage and held him there. "But, Coach, I didn't do anything," Swannie pleaded. When Frederick realized he might be telling the truth, he pushed him a little harder and said, "Well, okay...but this is for the times that you *did* do something and I missed it."

1974 CENTRAL WASHINGTON STATE COLLEGE BASEBALL
Won 23   Lost 11
Evergreen Conference Champions
2nd District #1

First Row: Taylor, Ted: (2nd team all-conference); Swanson, Jim, Fish, Bud, (2nd team all-conference,
             1st team all-district, captain; Mark Maxfield, (1st team all-conference, Steve Orrell Memorial
             Award; Wasson, Gary.
Second Row: Spencer, Jim (Hon. Men. all-conference, set school assist record); Gorton, Ty, (1st team all-
             conference, all district, all Pacific Coast, Hon. Mention All-American, Inspirational Award,
             Leading hitter on the team); Melton, Bill; Robinett, John; Stewart, Darryl; White, Neal;
             Feroglia, Casey;
Third Row: Hansen, Jeff; Arnold, Wayne; Fletcher, Tom; Easley, Rex; Kalian, Gregg, (1st team all-
             conference, all district, broke the school homerun record with 8); Clem, Jim; Dickey, Mike;
Back Row: Frederick, Gary, (Coach); Canfield, Dave, (Manager); Tinnell, Sonny; Boruff, Tom; LaForest,
             John; Hagan, Mike; Not pictured: Lettermen Hopkins, Don; Thomas, Jim; Nordlund, Chris.

(photo: CWU)

**CWU Team with Coach Frederick: back left, and
Swannie, front row, 2nd from left**

In his last year at Central, Swannie continued with the hot bat and solid fielding. He even convinced Coach Frederick to let him catch a game. Swanson responded by throwing out two baserunners and hitting a homer. He finished his career at Central with a .358 batting average and was selected to the All-Conference team in 1974.

Swannie graduated from Central with a degree in Business Education but didn't think he would need to be looking for a job anytime soon. Both he and his coach thought he would be in some round of the '75 MLB draft. After graduation, he returned home, stayed with his parents, and waited to see which Major League Baseball franchise would pick him up.

It turned out to be an agonizing time. When the days started slipping by without any calls from potential agents, Swannie started checking the phone for a dial tone every day. "Hello?"...click, click, "Anybody out there?"

When the draft came and went without a call, Swannie wandered around the house trying to come to grips that maybe his days of playing baseball were over. "What happened here?" he asked himself. "How come nobody called me? Did someone make a mistake?" It occurred to him that maybe he should try to remember what it was that he studied at Central Washington University.

In hindsight, many people may have made a mistake. Especially when you learn that the MLB draft choices that year had names like Filkens, Rosinski, O'Keefe, Benton, Barnicle, Miles, Johnson, Moretto, Welborn, Knapp, and Goodwin...and those were all *number one* draft choices! Probably all nice guys, sure, but hardly household names, except maybe in their own houses. In fact, in even hinder-sight, baseball historians tell us that the 1975 baseball draft was the weakest in history by far. With all that information, you'd thought that the draft would have had room for at least one player named Swanson.

Swannie's dad watched his son's anguish until he couldn't stand it anymore. He finally approached his son and said, "If you've got your heart set on playing baseball, you might wanna try out for that minor league club in Portland."

"Which one is that, Dad?"
"You know. The Mavericks."

CHAPTER SEVEN

Professional Baseball first came to the city of Portland, Oregon, in 1903, the same year that the Pacific Coast League was formed. The PCL was considered a Class AAA Minor League, just one notch below the Majors. The teams in the original PCL included the Sacramento Solons, Seattle Rainiers, Los Angeles Angels, Oakland Oaks, San Francisco Seals and the Portland Beavers.

Those of you that are paying attention might notice that the only cities on the aforementioned list, yet to be absorbed by Major League expansion, are Sacramento and Portland. Another interesting tidbit was that before expansion, the St. Louis Cardinals were both the westernmost *and* southernmost MLB team in the US.

After the 1971 season, The Portland Beavers, a franchise of the Cleveland Indians at the time, decided that the people in the Portland area weren't interested enough in Triple A baseball to support their team any longer so they packed up and moved to Spokane, Washington.

To say there were no baseball fans in the Portland area at the time would be unfair, after all, the city of Portland had supported a team at some level in every year but 1918. But the Beavers hadn't won anything close to a championship in thirty years. Perhaps people were just tired of dull, losing baseball? *Duh? Hellllooo?*

Whatever the cause for the Beavers fleeing their den, it looked like there would be no more boys of summer in Portland for the foreseeable future.

But then, in the nick of time, a new sheriff rode into town. His name was Bing Russell and he knew a thing or two about law and disorder.

Born Neil Oliver Russell, Bing was a talented actor probably best known for his role as Deputy Sheriff Clem Foster, on TV episodes of Bonanza. He played many other roles including heavies, and by his own account, he was killed-off over a hundred and twenty-three times.

Bing sang on Broadway and acted in numerous Hollywood movies, including one of the sequels of *The Magnificent Seven, The Apple Dumpling Gang, and Overboard,* a comedy which starred his son, Kurt and Goldie Hawn. Bing loved his craft and was damn good at it. He never lacked for work for any length of time. Bing was also a likable and friendly man who went through life with a one-word motto; 'fun'!

Another thing Bing was passionate about was baseball. When he was nine years old and living in St. Petersburg, Florida, he would hang out at the New York Yankees practice facility. One day he outraced several other kids for a foul ball and then had to fight them off to keep it. Lefty Gomez, the Yankee's ace lefty happened to see the boys scuffling and grabbed Bing by the collar and said, "Come with me, kid, I'll see to it that you never have to fight for a baseball the rest of your life."

Since Bing was being home-schooled, he was able to travel, and he spent the next eight years with the Yankees and was in the dugout for six World Series. He wasn't an official bat boy or even a clubhouse assistant, but the players liked having him the dugout, maybe for good luck, or more likely, as an errand boy. Because manager Joe McCarthy didn't want his players eating during games, some of the players engaged young Bing to sneak hot dogs and snacks to them.

One of Bing's fondest memories was when Lou Gehrig hit a home run in an exhibition game against the Brooklyn Dodgers. After rounding the bases, Gehrig took the bat that he had used to hit the homer and handed it to Bing in the dugout. It was the last home run that Gehrig would ever hit. The bat remained in the Russell family for years before fetching $400,000 in an auction. In 1973, when Bing heard that the rights to bring a new team into Portland could be purchased for $5,000, he almost jumped at the chance. And as it were, there was an actors' strike in Hollywood at the time, and Bing was bored. The opportunity to save baseball in Portland also gave Bing a chance to play a role he had always wanted: that of an owner of a professional baseball team. Although Bing had an interest in a Class AA team in El Paso, the idea of owning an *independent* team, (no bosses!) was too much to resist. In this case, it was only a Single A team that played an 80-game season in the Northwest League, but hey, it was a baseball team, right? How many people do you know that could say they owned a professional baseball team? Of course, Bing wasn't one to let it bother him that he didn't have the integral parts for a team at the moment, you know, like players and stuff.

But, being the good husband and father that he was, before he pulled the trigger on the deal, Bing talked it over with his family. Bing's wife, Louise was a gentle soul who had seen all the characters he had ever played, and knew the character that he forever was. She understood that there was probably no stopping him anyway, so she offered her support if he should choose to buy the rights to a baseball team.

But it was his son, Kurt, who was twenty-five at the time, who really saw that his dad needed to purge-the-urge and go for greatness. "Dad, you should get that team," he told him. "Whatever we run into you will figure it out. How tough can it be? You are way sharper than those guys wearing the suits, and you know baseball. Give it a chance."

Kurt Russell began *his* acting career at about the time the delivery doctor spanked his butt on March 17, 1951. The list of Kurt's TV and film credits is as long as his dads, *and*, like his dad and great-grandfather, Kurt loved baseball and was good enough to play the game professionally. In 1971, Kurt was signed by the Los Angeles Angels organization. Unfortunately, he suffered a devastating injury to his arm while turning a double play in a minor league game that pretty much ended his chances of making it to the Majors.

But Kurt still had a burning desire to play baseball so when his father and John Carbray founded the Portland Mavericks, Kurt played second base as much as he could between acting gigs. He would later say, "Movies are only a part of my life. Baseball is the complete experience. I had three sisters in real life, but I had a thousand brothers in baseball."

Fortunately for movie fans, Kurt never gave up his day job and still does pretty well with it, bad rotator cuff and all.

Six months after creating the Mavericks, Bing bought out Carbray and became sole owner of the team.

(photo: Sue Swanson)

Kurt Russell as Maverick #28

CHAPTER EIGHT

In the early going, Kurt played an important role in the Mavericks, 'organization' by finding guys to play for the team. He took out ads in the local papers and made phone calls. "Hi, my name's Kurt Russell and I'm wondering if you know anybody that can play baseball and would like to try out for our club?"

Meanwhile, his dad visited bars, pool halls and restaurants, introducing himself and recruiting players as he went. Many people started to wonder if what Bing was doing was even legal. *Don't you have to take a test or something before you can own and fabricate a professional baseball team? Isn't there a criterion that pro players must meet, like being able to actually catch or hit a baseball? Can just anybody walk on and play?*

Local fans and sportswriters weren't sure what was going on. *Who is this guy and what's he trying to pull? Some relative of B.T. Barnum? He's from Hollywood, right?*

Anybody in the hierarchy of professional baseball knew that what Bing Russel was doing was not how things were supposed to be done. Nobody puts ads in papers for professional baseball players. This was not a high school turnout. Open casting calls for players? *Really?* It must be some kind of a joke, some kind of a scam on the people of Portland. After all, being an Independent team in this league meant playing against farm clubs that were owned by a Major League team. Major League franchises didn't have walk-ons, their players had *agents.* They had incentive contracts. They all had nice uniforms that their mothers didn't have to wash.

But somehow, Bing eventually put it all together and signed thirty misfits, vagabonds, rookies, has-beens, construction workers, bartenders, and semi-pro somethings. For his first manager, Bing hired a friend and a fellow actor named Hank Robinson.

Robinson had seventy-six film and television credits on his resume. Everything from the Bob Newhart Show, Rockford Files, Fantasy Island, Bonanza and Batman to Airplane II, The Godfather, Blazing Saddles, and The Naked Gun.

In fact, it may have been Robinson's role in the 'Naked Gun' that landed him the job with Bing. In the movie, Robinson played the role of an umpire, which in Bing's mind qualified him as a manager for a team called The Mavericks.

Bing even held tryouts for batboy and batgirl. Of course, Bing's own experience as a kid in the dugout undoubtedly influenced his decision to hold tryouts for that position. One of his wiser decisions was selecting a boy by the name of Todd Field. Bing must have sensed the potential in the youngster because years later, Field became an actor himself and as of this writing, as earned three Academy Award nominations as a writer and director. Todd Field would also become the only batboy to ever be thrown out of a game (more on that later). Bing was immensely proud of the young lad.

Bing later hired a young woman named Lanny Moss to be his general manager, making her the first professional female GM in baseball. Moss was just 22 years old, a minister's daughter whose work experience included working as a switchboard operator for the Salvation Army in Portland. In 1974, Russell told *The Spokane Review,* "The fact that she's a girl has nothing to do with the simple premise that I wanted her for the job. She's much tougher with a dollar than I am."

Some folks suggested that one of the reasons Bing hired Moss was her work experience in Portland and how it might come in handy for recruiting purposes.

Later, Bing scored another first by hiring the first Asian-American general manager in baseball. You could say that Bing was the epitome of 'equal opportunity employer' for all races, gender, and age groups.

On June 22, 1973, the Portland Mavericks played their first ever game against the Walla Walla Padres, an affiliate of the San

Diego Padres. The Mavericks' starting pitcher was a young man named Gene Lanthom, who followed a script straight out of Hollywood. Lanthom threw a no-hitter, and the Mavs won the game 4-0. For the Portland Mavericks, it was 'game on'!

CHAPTER NINE

In June of '75, Swannie went with his Dad to Civic Stadium in Portland to try out for the Mavericks. The stadium was crowded with wannabees of every description; young, old, fat, skinny, short, tall, black, white, brown, red, long hair, beards, bald, clean shaven, buzz cuts, some handsome, some not so handsome.

It was painfully obvious that Bing Russell was still recruiting players from bars and pool halls, but by this time his club had established itself in the league as a team to be reckoned with. In their inaugural year they finished second in their league with a record of 45-35. The next year they finished second again, improving to 50-34. They were beating the franchise clubs that were bringing up players like Ozzie Smith, Ricky Henderson, Dave Henderson, Dave Stewart, Mike Scioscia, and Pedro Guerrero. The Mavs were having fun and drawing good crowds. That meant they also drew the attention of a lot of guys who wanted to make the club and join the merriment. The day that Swannie turned out for the team, there were about three hundred other guys wanting to join the fray. It was going to be a long day.

Everybody trying out that day was given a number to wear on their back, something you might see on the back of track runners...or livestock. The coaches and assistants first lined up players to take a few cuts at the plate while sending the others to whatever position they were trying out for. The pitchers were sent to designated areas to throw, while one of the pitching coaches threw to the batter. The idea was to simulate a real game. After the batter took his cuts, he became a base runner before eventually taking his place in the infield or outfield. Most anybody that grew up playing baseball probably played a similar type of game called 'workup'.

With so many players to look at, the hitters were only given a few pitches on the first go-round. Swannie was one of the first batters up and did okay by stinging a couple pitches to right field. Then, before he really felt warmed up, he became a base runner and was eventually was rotated to the outfield. Our man was a little nervous, almost miss-played the first ball hit to him, but after that he settled in and did just fine.

After his stint in the field, Swannie joined his father and sat in the stands to watch the rest of the competition. As player after player took their turn batting and fielding, Swannie grew more and more discouraged. Even though he felt he was better than most of the guys he was watching, the odds just seemed stacked against him. Some of the players trying out seemed to be chummy with the coaches and shared a few laughs.

Swannie knew no one other than the man next to him. "We might as well go home, Dad," Swannie said. This ain't workin'. Too many other guys."

His father just looked at him and said, "Too many guys in the outfield maybe, but I only see a couple of players with a catcher's glove on."

Earle reached down into the equipment bag that he had brought and pulled out Swannie's catcher's mitt. "Here, go show 'em what else you got."

Swannie took the glove and his dad's advice and approached one of the coaches that was conducting the infield tryouts. Before Swannie even said a word, the coach noticed Swannie was carrying a catcher's mitt. What he didn't notice was that it was a *left-handed* catcher's mitt.

"You tryin' out for catcher?" The coach asked. "Yes, sir." Swannie said.

"Okay. We'll put you behind the plate after the next batter."

When it was his turn to catch, the first thing Swannie did was throw out the runner trying to steal second. After the next batter finished his cuts and rotated to become a runner, Swannie picked him off of first base. This went on for several batters until someone came out of the dugout and yelled, "Wait a minute. Timeout!" It was Bing Russell.

He walked up to the plate and looked at Swannie. "You're left-handed!"

"Really?" Swannie answered, ever the wise-ass. "My father mentioned that, too."

"There's no such thing as a left-handed catcher in baseball!" Bing declared.

"He didn't mention that part."

Bing looked at the coach, "Did you know he was left-handed?"

"Well, I---"

"That's okay, never mind. He's perfect! He's a maverick. Sign him up!"

Bing slapped Swannie on the back and then stuck out his hand to shake on the deal. Swannie's hand shot out, forgetting for a moment that he was left-handed catcher with a glove on his right hand. Bing laughed and waited patiently while Swannie struggled to take his glove off.

Thus, began the professional baseball career of Jim Swanson, our man Swannie.

CHAPTER TEN

As the great Yogi Berra once said, "When you come to a fork in the road, take it." Swannie wasn't aware of it at the time but the minute he put on his catcher's mitt and made the Mavericks baseball team, his life was changed forever. It would be one of the defining moments of his time. Not because he went on to have a great baseball career, which he didn't, but because of the things he was about to experience in the next three years with the Mavs.

Besides the uniqueness of a left-handed catcher, Bing Russell was also looking for a really good utility man. Someone that could play every position in the outfield. A man that could sit behind the plate. A man that could pinch-hit as well as pinch-run. A guy that could keep the team loose in the locker room. These are all good qualities in a standard utility man, of course, but the Bingster was looking to get even more out of the position. He wanted a guy that could handle the loudspeaker on the bus. He wanted a player that could take care of hotel check-ins. He wanted someone that could serve as a bodyguard for the team manager, including at times, providing protection for the manager from his own players. He wanted a professional game interrupter, someone who could let their mascot, a black labby-looking dog named P.L. Maverick, loose in the field when the opposing pitcher was on a roll. He was looking for a scrapper who could start a fight when needed. And, he was looking for a player that could tell another player that he was no longer needed by the club. Somehow, Bing saw all of that in Swannie.

The first sniff of what was in store for Swannie came during the second day of tryouts, after he had made the team. Bing was in the dugout, studying a list he held in his hands. He called Swannie over to him and said, "Okay, son, here's what I want you to do. I want you to go out to right field for a while."

34

"Sure," Swannie said, and grabbed his mitt.

"Wait. You won't need your glove. Here, take this bat instead. I want you out there by the exit tunnel."

"Ah...okay. But what am I doin'?"

"Earning your stripes for one thing. As the day goes on, I'll be sending some guys out there to talk to you."

"What about?"

"About their not making this team." "Huh?"

"The guys will come out to see you a few at a time and they'll have all their gear with them. They've been cut from the team but they just don't know it yet. When they get to you, I want you to thank them for coming out, invite them to try out again next year if they want to, then point them to the exit."

"Really?"

"Really. I just don't want anybody coming back here making a scene."

"Hmm." Swannie took a cut with the bat, looked at Bing, and then trotted out to right field. What the hell, he was a professional.

(photo: Sue Swanson)

Swannie Pointing the Way

Terry Cubbins

CHAPTER ELEVEN

By the time Swannie joined the Mavericks, former manager Hank Robinson had been suspended for a year by the league for punching an umpire in the face. Robinson, who was just in his second year as skipper, admitted he was wrong to hit the ump but since the guy pushed him a couple of times first, Robinson felt he had no choice but to defend himself.

Bing Russell thought the one-year suspension was too harsh and stuck up for his friend, but the league was adamant. Bing didn't want to fire Robinson, but in the end, he realized he had to let him go. Robinson returned to Hollywood and told his agent that he would accept more roles as an umpire since he now had first-hand experience with them.

Bing was looking for a new manager when he got a call from a local sportswriter who suggested that Bing talk to a man called Frank 'The Flake' Peters. Peters owned and managed a bar in Portland called Peters Inn where sportswriters liked to hang out.

Peters had gotten started in the bar business by working as a bartender at Pudgy Hunt's Bottle Shop near Lloyd Center in Portland. It was busy joint where local hockey players could be found carousing. Peters made $2.85 an hour and felt he was wildly overpaid.

*Hmm...*Bing thought. *Let's see, bar owner?...check. Manager?...check. Hangout for sportswriters?...check. Works cheap?...check. 'The Flake'?...check, check.*

Bing soon arranged to meet with Peters for an interview at Peters Inn. Bing's thinking was even if the hire didn't work out, maybe he would spot a recruit or two and schmooze some sportswriters at the same time.

But, when the two met, Bing knew he had his next manager. Frank Peters was a tall, lanky, athletic, blond-haired, blue-eyed, thirty-ish, smiley, rakish, single man with a give-a-shit attitude and a penchant for the booze and babes. However, he could also be a disciplinarian when needed. His personality could be described as somewhere between George Patton's and Gene Wilder's.

Actually, Peters may have been overqualified for the job. Besides being a free spirit, he had been a very good athlete himself and had played on Oregon State's 1962-63 basketball team that reached the NCAA final four. His teammates included future NBA player, Mel Counts, and Terry Baker, the football star who won the 1962 Heisman Trophy.

Peters also played college baseball as a third baseman and hit with a high average. In his junior year he quit school to sign with the Baltimore Orioles, where he was assigned to their AAA franchise in Rochester, New York. Only problem was, the Orioles already had a guy that could play third pretty well himself, fella by the name of Brooks Robinson. All in all, Peters played Minor League ball for five different teams in ten years, three of those years for his beloved Portland Beavers.

As a kid, Peters grew up dreaming about someday playing for the Portland Beavers. In fact, it may have been during his time with the club that Peters began earning the nickname, "The Flake". Case in point; once when he was about to be traded from the Portland Beavers to the Tacoma Twins, Peters scraped up enough money to negotiate a deal with the Tacoma club that would nix the trade and leave Peters in Portland. In Peters' words, "I think I'm the only one in baseball that ever traded for himself."

When he wasn't riding his shiny black Harley-Davidson, Peters drove a bright red Cadillac and lived on a houseboat. These nuances don't automatically qualify someone as a flake per se, especially during the 70's, but in Peters' case, enough of these characteristics were like snowflakes that fell and stuck.

Peter's baseball managing style definitely helped establish his nickname as well.

When he took over the club, his first rule was, "There are no rules. No signals either." If Swannie had been expecting to play for a manager who had scruples and really knew his craft, he was about to be set straight. Let's just say Swannie was about to take a detour from the teachings of Father O'Brien and Coach Frederick.

Where Father O'Brien might say, "Stick to the straight and narrow son, and trust in God. He will take care of you," Bing Russell said, "Stick with me, kid, I'll show you the real world."

Where Coach Frederick would say, "If I catch you smoking, you're off the team." Frank 'The Flake' Peters, said, "Pot smokers sit in the back of the bus."

The Mavericks' bus itself was a sight to behold. It was an old school bus painted the same colors as the Mavs uniform, 'street walker red'. On each side of the bus in black paint was the lettering, 'Portland's Maverick Baseball Team.' The apostrophe and 's' at the end of *Portland* had been mistakenly painted in, but when Bing realized the mistake, he felt it captured the essence of the team even better, so he left it there.

On top of the bus, Bing had mounted a loudspeaker and rigged a P.A. system so when the bus rolled into a rival town, a designated player/announcer of the day (see utility player) would broadcast warnings to everyone on the street. "Hey, hey, hey, here come the big bad Mavericks! Batten down the hatches! Lock your doors! Lock up your sisters, wives, and mothers too!! We're here to kick some butt!"

The seats in the back of the bus had been taken out and replaced with mattresses on the floor. An overhead light had been rigged up so the players could roll joints better and see the cards they were playing.

Like sailors on shore leave, the Mavs seemed to gravitate toward trouble when they were on the road. The red bus was their ship, and any town that they were playing in became their port of call.

Keeping with his equal opportunity hiring policy, Bing hired a low key, middle-aged lady to drive the bus. For one thing, he knew she had much more experience in driving a school bus than any of his players, and, maybe her presence behind the wheel would help keep his boys from getting too far out of line. *Sure, Bing.*

CHAPTER TWELVE

As soon as Frank Peters teamed up with Bing Russell, Peters knew he had a future in the entertainment business as well as baseball.

Now, everybody knows that baseball is a sport. A sport that most boys and girls grew up playing for fun. But when players started getting paid to play, an entertainment factor entered the picture. Nobody knew this more than Bing Russell, after all, he was a professional entertainer himself. A real showman. If you're paid to entertain people, you damn well better do your job, or you won't have it much longer. And like all good directors and choreographers, he knew that for the act to work, the stars as well as the entire supporting cast would have to know their parts well and buy in to the story.

That story line became the culture for the Mavs. They were a bunch of players with attitudes. They were usually older than the players on the franchise teams, but they all liked to win. They were also somewhat enigmatic. They didn't conform with regimented behavior or appearances. They were vagabonds. They liked to have fun but were fiercely competitive at the same time. They knew that this might be their last hurrah. Reggie Thomas, for instance, was drafted in 1965 by the Houston Astros in the 72nd round. He kicked around Single A ball for eight years, mostly playing the outfield, before joining the Mavs in 1973. He was an extremely fast base runner and was often compared to Maury Wills. In fact, Thomas was so fast that many times when he hit what looked like a sure double, he would stop at first just so he could later steal second and add to his stolen base totals.

But Thomas was explosive in more ways than one. When he first joined the club and looked through the Mavs lineup, he crowned himself the star. But that was just fine with Bing and

Peters because they felt the man would play his part just fine, thank you.

In a move to ensure that Thomas felt comfortable in his status as the headliner, Bing set him up in an apartment just a block and a half from Civic Stadium. Before each game, a car was sent to pick up Thomas so he wouldn't have to walk all that way to the park. Maybe Bing was saving Thomas' strength for the base paths?

Bing knew from the get-go that the baseball team he was putting together wouldn't be able to survive on smoke and mirrors, or juggling acts for long, or they'd soon be out of business (see Portland Beavers). His Independent team would be going up against Major League franchises and Bing didn't just want to be competitive, he wanted to knock the shit out of the other teams. And to win ballgames with all walk-ons was going to be a huge challenge.

But Bing was up to that challenge. He knew that for most of his players, this was their last chance to make it in professional baseball. They couldn't go any lower than Single A unless they went semi-pro. (The Mavericks' salaries could almost qualify as semi-pro as players were paid an average salary of $300 a month!) Bing used this to motivate his players. "If you can't play at this level, you can't play at all. You want to realize your dream, don't you? You want to show your friends and family you can play, right? You want to prove it to yourself, too. I know you do. And I'm telling you right now, if every one of you digs deep and gives me all they got, we can win here. And you'll continue to do what you love to do, and that's play baseball."

Not sure if Bing ever played the role of a snake-oil salesman in the movies, but he did a damn fine job of convincing each of his players if they drank his concoction, they were bound for glory!

Bing's plan was to field a team that believed they could walk on hot coals and sing at the same time. He fed his team mental steroids, hoping they could intimidate other teams with their bravado. They would be like Muhammad Ali dancing around the ring, feinting left and right, frustrating opponents into swinging wildly. Bing understood Ali's strategy often consisted of getting his opponent out of their comfort zone.

One of Ali's favorite tricks-of-the-trade was to be near his own corner when the bell was about to ring to end the round. Ali would do a little shuffle, bop the other guy in the nose, "Here." *Pow!* "Take this wit you." Ali would then sit down immediately on his stool, which gave him a couple of extra seconds to rest. It also gave the other guy something to think about on his long walk back across the ring to his own corner.

Bing employed psychology in every way he could. During one mild losing stretch when the Mavs needed to refocus, Bing decided not to charge fans going *into* Civic Stadium, instead, asking them to pay whatever they thought the game was worth, on their way *out*. It worked. The team began winning again. He had challenged his player's pride and psyche and dared them to put the chips back on their collective shoulders.

When Peters took over as manager, he was smart enough to see that the Mavs' culture was already established and it was just flakey enough for him to roll right with it. In fact, one day in his early going and the Mavs in a bit of a slump, Peters decided a change was in order. Well, not just one change. Nine of them. During one game, Peters shifted every player to another position to start each inning. All the players ended up playing all nine positions on the field.

After the team lost that game, Peters was asked if he was worried about what Bing might have thought about the strategy.

"Not at all," he said. "It's like Bing and I are on the same horse, him on the front and me on the back."

In 1974, the year Peters was hired as manager, Bing Russell was named the Class A Executive of the Year. At the award ceremony, Bing was presented his trophy by none other than his old-time mentor, Vernon Louis Gomez, aka "Lefty" Gomez.

For those of you that are under forty or were born at night in Russia, Lefty Gomez was a perennial All-Star pitcher with the Yankees from 1933-1938. and, yes, he was left-handed. Despite their age difference, Bing and Lefty shared some things in common.

Lefty's wife was in show business and appeared on Broadway. Bing of course was an entertainer and had performed on the Great White Way for years.

Bing was widely known by a nickname, and so was Lefty. Gomez was also known as 'El Goofo', which could have fit Bing just as well. Both men liked practical jokes and each had a great sense of humor, both on and off the diamond.

Some of Bing's antics have been covered in this story, but an example of Lefty's humor showed up one day in a game when he was pitching against Bob Feller, a fastball pitcher who wasn't afraid to throw inside to a batter. It had been foggy most of that day and was getting worse when Lefty came up to the plate to face 'Rapid Robert'. Just before he stepped into the batter's box, Lefty lit a match and held it up. The umpire asked him, "You think that'll help you see his fastball?"

"Hell no," Lefty said, "I just wanna make sure he can *see me*."

Gomez was also known to brush hitters back off of the plate from time to time and was once asked by a reporter, "Is it true you would throw at your own mother?" Lefty replied, "Damn right I would. She's a good hitter!"

When Lefty Gomez presented Bing Russel with the Executive-of-the-Year Award, Bing said, "This is one of my proudest moments of my life. Not just for the trophy itself, but the fact that I'm standing here with my hero to receive it."

CHAPTER THIRTEEN

There were not-always-proud moments in and around the Mavericks' traveling circus. As was the case when they took their trusty bus to Walla Walla, Washington to play a game against the Walla Walla Padres. The Mavs arrived late afternoon the day before the game and checked into the Marcus Whitman Hotel, a grand historical hotel built in the 1920's.

After they stored their gear, a few of the newer players migrated down to the hotel's bar and grabbed a table. There were about a dozen other people scattered around the room, chatting and enjoying happy hour. Frank Peters was not among them which didn't surprise anyone, because Peters had once paraphrased the great Casey Stengel, "Make sure the people that hate your guts are separated from the ones that haven't made up their minds yet."

As happy hour turned into an even happier hour, a lovely young lady strolled in alone and made herself comfortable at the bar. By this time, the players had drunk enough to think that they were taller and better looking than they used to be. As time passed and the gal still sat alone smoking a cigarette, Swannie got up and stumbled over to the bar and took a shot at her.

"Hey. You're probably wonderin' what a good-lookin' guy like me is doin' in a joint like this, huh?"

The young woman smiled at him. "No, not really. But I can ask my boyfriend when he gets here, okay?" She took a drag off of her cigarette and blew smoke in Swannie's face.

Swannie stood there trying to think of something clever to say, but the only sound that came out of his mouth was a burp. Red-faced and pissed, he turned and slithered his way back to his table and sat down.

"Nice hit, Swannie," one of his pals needled. Another said in an announcer's voice, "A swing and a miss...he's outta dare!"

Everyone in the room seemed to be enjoying the act.

Swannie quickly tossed back his drink. If he was learning anything about professional baseball, it was the drinking part.

"Big deal. She ain't that hot up close." Swannie said. "She thinks she's a looker but she juss don know class when she sees it." Swannie waved his arm at the bartender. "Lesh' have another round here."

The bartender took his time with the drinks and when he finally brought them over to the table, he also brought a bar menu. "You guys had anything to eat today? How about some appetizers?"

As one of them looked over the menu, Swannie got up and said, "I gotta pee. Order me somthin'. I'll be right back."

Swannie left the bar and took a short walk down a hallway looking for the men's room. Except for the nameplate that said 'Gentlemen' above one of doors, all of the doors looked the same.

It could have been the nameplate on the door that threw Swannie, or maybe he was having trouble seeing, but for whatever reason, he missed the men's room and walked right on by it. He kept going until he came to the end of the hallway which led him either left or right. Confused, he looked back down the way he came. That's when he saw the woman from the bar. She didn't look his way, but she walked straight across the hallway and up a short flight of stairs.

"Hey!" Swandog hurried down the hall, turned, and took the steps two at a time. He reached the top of the stairs just as the woman was entering a door.

"Hey," he yelled again.

She looked over her shoulder, let herself in, and quickly shut the door.

Swannie reached her door and gave it a couple of raps. "Hey! How 'bout a little help here? I'm trying..."

"Go away!" "I gotta pee." "Tough shit!"

"...but I can't find the men's room." "So? Go pee in your own room!!" "I don't know where that is either."

"Tough shit. Go away! I'm calling security."

"What?" Swannie was holding on to himself now. "No, wait. Really. You don't understand...I jus...I...jus really have to pee!"

"Not in here you don't!" The lady said. The next sound Swannie heard was made by a deadbolt being closed; *ker-klack!*

Swannie looked down at the door handle and lock. It was one of the old-fashioned kinds that offered a keyhole, the kind that you used to be able to see through. Swannie bent over and put an eyeball to the keyhole. *Viola!* He *could* see through it, but not enough to tell what was going on in the room.

When he stood up and looked at the door, he realized the keyhole was just about pecker level. *Umm, if I can see through it, I can pee through it!*

Without further ado, Swannie unzipped and freed Willy. With one hand he leaned against the door and used his other hand to guide Willy to the keyhole. He did have to stand slightly on his toes, but when he felt he was aimed properly, he let go and peed...and peed...and peed. He kept peeing until he farted.

Feeling greatly relieved, Swannie heard the woman yelling and decided that finding his own room might be his next move. He turned the corner just as hotel security was arriving at the scene.

The next morning Frank Peters called for a team meeting at nine o'clock in the hotel's restaurant. Most of the players were wondering what it was all about because Peter's didn't usually call for team meeting unless it was right *after* a game when he wanted to rant about players performances. He had also made it clear that he didn't care much about what the team did on their own time as long as they showed up to play on game day. So, why the meeting at the ungodly hour of 9:00 am?

With everybody seated in the restaurant, Peter's strode into the meeting tapping a very large steak knife against his leg. He stopped at the nearest table and used the knife to clink a pitcher of water, effectively calling the meeting to order.

"While I was out last night with some local sportswriters, trying to promote today's game so you fuckheads can stay in business, one of you thought it would be funny to piss through the keyhole of my hotel room door. I'm telling you right now that I didn't care for that at all. My girlfriend was in the room at the time and it made her mad as hell! She had to call security."

Peters looked around the tables, letting his words sink in. Some of the players were trying not to smile, others looked at the ceiling. Finally, Peters spoke again, "While I'm not adverse to you bozos having a little fun, I have to tell you that my girlfriend left the hotel last night and found another place to sleep. And that means *I* didn't have any fun last night. You get my drift?"

Nobody answered of course, just more suppressed smiles and a few coughs.

Peter's slapped the steak knife against the palm of his hand. "I was going to find the guy that did it and *peen*alize him, but then I realized that anybody with a wee-wee small enough to fit in a keyhole, has probably been punished enough in life.

"And speaking of wee-wees, do any of you know what Walla Walla means in Indian?

It means small river. You see, Walla, means river, and in Indian, if you say the same word twice it diminishes the first word."

Peters looked at Swannie and pointed the knife at him. "You got that, Dick Dick?"

CHAPTER FOURTEEN

One of the qualities of a good manager is the ability to forgive and forget. Peters had that ability, especially when it would serve him well to do so. Swannie got back on Peters' good side when he earned the role as his bodyguard. It happened one evening at a team party. The club had just won a game that put them in first place, and they were celebrating accordingly. Of course, the Mavs never needed an excuse to party, but winning a game always gave them an extra kick.

The celebration had been going on for about an hour when one of the Mavs decided Peters wasn't giving him enough credit for the victory that day. When Peters turned his back, the player picked up a chair to throw at Peters. Swannie saw what was happening and warned Peters to duck.

Later that evening, Peters graciously acknowledged that Swannie had probably saved his life, and for that, Swannie would be awarded the job of guarding Peters' body for the rest of the season. Swannie, being the professional that he was, accepted the position as part of being a Maverick.

Swannie wasn't your typical bodyguard or muscle. He didn't always walk in front of Peters, didn't wear shades constantly, didn't pack heat, never wore a wire in his ear, and the only black belt he owned kept his pants up. Swannie's role was more of a vocal alert system to Peters. Swannie's strong suit was enunciating clearly, distinguishing the difference between words like, 'fuck and duck'.

Swannie's uncanny feel for when other Maverick players had had enough of Peters' crap and wanted to kick the shit out of him. Swannie's radar came into play again after the Mavs had just lost a close game in Bellingham. The team had returned to their hotel and Peters called for a team meeting in the bar. He was particularly upset with some of the mental mistakes that a couple of guys made that may have cost them the game.

Peters lit into Terry Lee, a first-round draft choice who played shortstop. Swannie remembers the encounter well and what Peters said. "When you got on first base in the fourth, with two outs and the count went oh-and-two on Cervantes, why in hell didn't you try to steal second? You got a righty on the mound. You know he's not gonna give Cervantes a good pitch to hit, and for those of you that are mentally challenged, that means that the pitcher probably isn't gonna give his catcher anything good to catch either! Probably something outside. And, if you *do* get thrown out, big deal, so what? Cervantes leads off the next inning with a fresh count. Use your fuckin' head man!"

Of course, nobody is in a good mood after losing a game and Peters' habit of calling meetings afterward to harangue his players was getting on a lot of nerves. Everything Peters was saying was simple baseball acumen, but the tone of his voice and the way he was presenting his point was irksome. Soon, Terry Lee had had enough.

"Yeah, right, Frank!" Lee stood up and yelled. "And maybe if we were all fuckin' geniuses like you, we would know better! Okay? Or, maybe, just maybe, if we had something like... *signs?* You know? They're like signals, but they're called *signs?*... From *coaches?*... Then maybe we would know when you wanted us to fucking steal a fuckin' base or not!!"

Peters was already on his feet and about ready to get nose to nose with Lee when Swannie went into bodyguard mode. He jumped between the two and placed the palm of his hand on Peters' chest. Peters broke off his stare-down with Lee long enough to look down at the hand on his chest. Incredulously he looked at Swannie. "Why are you touching me, you little shit?"

Swannie, never one to back down from anyone, said, "Well, Frank, I'm sorta wondering about that right now myself. But since you pay me extra money to do it, I'm doin' it."

Peters' bushy eyebrows knotted and his jawbone twitched as he glared at Swannie for a couple of seconds. But slowly, his countenance reluctantly changed from anger to remembrance as he looked at his catcher. *Oh, yeah. Okay.*

Swannie had done his job once more. He nodded at Lee and moved his hand and patted Peters' shoulder. "C'mon Frank. Let's go over to the bar across the street and I'll kick your ass in a game of pool."

CHAPTER FIFTEEN

The place across the street was a small tavern named Ernie's. The place could handle about a dozen butts at the bar, while a couple of tables that surrounded a green felt pool table could seat a few more. There were about a six people at the bar and another six or so at the tables. The lone bartender was about fifty, five-eleven, black curly hair sprinkled with gray. He wore a starched white shirt with sleeves rolled up over beefy arms. He looked like an Ernie.

Swannie and Peters grabbed an empty table nearest the pool table where an older man and a somewhat younger woman were shooting a game of eight-ball. Before sitting down, Peters waved his hat and signaled the bartender for a pitcher of beer. There were guys at a nearby table who looked like they'd already had a few pitchers themselves.

One of them leaned in and said something to the others. To Swannie, it sounded like the guy said, *'fuckin' Mavericks hat!'* Peters didn't seem to notice so Swannie decided not to pass that info along to his boss/manager for the moment. Peters was still a little hot under the collar but the color in his face had returned to normal.

"Sometimes I think the team hates me." Peters said, after their beer arrived. "No shit? What makes you think so?" Swannie asked sarcastically.

"No, really. Listen. Sometimes I think they really do hate me." Peters said.

Swannie could see his boss needed a little compassion. "Oh, bullshit. That's not true and you know it. They...ah...well, you know...they...a... love you. Well, okay, maybe not all of them. And, not all of the time...but, you know..."

About that time the older gentleman that was shooting pool moved around the table to get in position for a shot. It put him right next to where Swannie and Peters were sitting. Peters politely leaned to one side to give the man room to shoot. The old man sighted down his stick and, like a nervous golfer taking way too many waggles, he kept drawing the pool cue back and forth, back and forth, getting ready for the real thing. As the seconds ticked by, Peters grew more uncomfortable holding his position and breath. Finally, the old man's practice-swishes stopped and he quickly pulled the trigger, sending the cue ball directly, and loudly, into the side pocket.

As the old man shuffled away, Peters returned to his full and upright position and muttered, "Nice shot, Fats."

The old man spun around, ('spun' being a relative term in this case) and glared at Peters. Peters just smiled as the old man turned and grumbled away.

Peters poured himself a beer and said to Swannie, "Another part of your job as bodyguard is to kill me if I ever get that old and senile, okay?"

"Sure boss, whatever you say."

F ifteen minutes and a pitcher of beer later, the same scenario took place. The old man was still playing and once again he had a shot that put him next to Swannie and Peters' table. He looked briefly at Peters before he took his position, and again Peters moved his upper body away to give the man room for his shot. The man started through his routine again; *sight down stick, look up at target ball, aim...practice stroke, swish, aim...look up at target ball, practice stroke...aim. Swish, swish.* Peters looked at Swannie for moral guidance, but Swannie just shrugged his shoulders. If there was ever a Rodney Dangerfield moment, this was it. *While we're young!*

Eventually, Peters' had had enough. As Gramps waggled the cue back for yet another practice stroke, Peters reached over and tapped the butt end of the stick. The old man yelped, and the cue ball 'clinked' weakly into the target ball, sending nothing nowhere. The woman let out a laugh.

"Goddamn you, " the old man yelled. He held the cue stick like a baseball bat and looked like he was about to take a swing with it.

Peters broke into laughter, which just pissed Gramps off even more.

"That's it you sumbitch!" Gramps yelled and swung his stick at Peters. Peters immediately stopped laughing and ducked as the cue stick whizzed just inches over his head. When the old man regained his balance and set up in a left-handed stance for another go, Peters jumped up, grabbed him by the shirt and belt, and threw him across the pool table. The old man rolled off the end of the table and fell on the floor, making sort of a 'whump' sound. The woman gasped something like... "ogah!"

The three guys at the other table immediately jumped up. One of them yelled,"Hey, what the fuck you think you're doin', asshole? He's an old man for Christ sakes!"

Peters answered in less than a heartbeat. "Yeah, so what? He tried to kill me with that cue stick! That's a weapon. *And,* he's crazy! That makes us the same age!"

The woman helped the old man off the floor as the bartender came running over. "Alright, break it up. What the hell's goin' on here?"

The guy from the other table said in a rage, "Ernie, this bozo here threw Fred across the fucking pool table! I think he's lookin' to get his ass kicked."

Peters gave the guy the finger, who answered by tossing some beer in Peters' direction.

Ernie quickly jumped in between the two. "Alright! That's it. Outta here, now! Nobody's kickin' nobody's ass in here. Take it outside, or I'll call the cops! Now!!"

When everyone, including the old man, started to go outside, Ernie realized his mistake. He grabbed Swannie by the arm. "Wait a minute. You two stay where you're at for now."

When one of the other men got even pissed-er, and questioned the call, Ernie waved him off, explaining, "They haven't paid their bill yet. You guys get outta here!"

Ernie took his own sweet time tallying the bill, figuring the other guys might get tired of waiting outside and leave. He took it a step further by leading Swannie and Peters to a back door. As he held the door open, he asked, "You guys play for the Mavericks, don't you?"

Both heads turned to Ernie, smiling they said, "As a matter of fact, we do."

Ernie nodded toward the darkness outside. "Then don't ever come in here again."

CHAPTER SIXTEEN

Swannie and Peters walked through an alley and around a corner to the main street. Peters didn't really want to go back to the hotel just yet, but Swannie talked him into it. "We probably have a bar tab to pay over there too." Swannie said. "Might as well take care of it while we're making so many friends."

Peters looked at Swannie and said, "Amigo, I don't think I have any friends right now."

"Sure you do, Frank. You just called *me* your friend."

They were halfway across the street when a light blue, four-door Chevy pulled away from the curb near their hotel. The car's bright lights came on and the driver suddenly gunned the engine, the car surging forward. One of the guys from the bar leaned out of the passenger side window and yelled, "No jay-walking, assholes!" It was obviously an attempt to scare Peters and Swannie, but as the car passed them, Swannie turned his back to the car and horse-kicked the rear fender, making a nice little 'whack' sound. The recoil of the kick sent Swannie into the curb, where he fell and cracked his head. The Chevy went a few feet before it stopped in the middle of the street. The three men jumped out and looked back at Swannie and then at the rear fender. One of them said to the driver, "You didn't hit him, he hit us. I saw him kick the car. Look, you can see his footprint, right there!"

Peters was helping Swannie to his feet when he yelled, "That's right fuckface! He kicked your god-damn car and I'll kick your fuckin' ass if you ever come near us again!!

Peters put his arm around his amigo and together they walked through the hotel's entrance and into the bar.

Most of the Mavericks were still sitting where Swannie and Peters had left them.

Terry Lee was the first to notice the blood trickling down Swannie's head. "Hey, what's with that?"

Meanwhile, the driver pulled the car over to the curb, joined his other stooges and together they headed to the hotel. When they got inside at the bar, they spotted Peters sitting at the nearest table, examining the back of Swannie's noggin. The driver of the car, who was also the biggest of the three, called out. "All right, which one of you fuckers is gonna pay for the dent in my car?" Peters stopped what he was doing and said, "How'd you like a dent in your head, you stupid shit?"

The posturing wasn't just for show, things were ramping up quickly on both sides. The driver fired back. "You think you're hot-shit because you play for the Portland-fucking-Mavericks? Big fucking deal. You suck and so does your team! Get up. Let's go!"

That was probably the stoogiest thing that driver-guy could have said. Apparently, he hadn't noticed the assortment of fellows sitting behind Swannie and Peters. The twenty-or-so, scowling, freaky-looking, drooling, beer-drinking guys, who were wearing batting helmets and Maverick baseball hats pointed in every direction; backwards, sideways, and inside-out.

There was a moment of stunned silence in the bar. Peters stood up. Two seconds later the rest of the Mavericks behind him did the same. Driver-guy's eyes widened and he said something, but it came out garbled. He puffed out his chest and started to nod his head like he was assessing the situation, like he didn't give a damn how many he was going to have to deal with. He stood there nodding, looking around, not saying anything, trying to look tough, but finally a gulp gave him away. Without another attempt at communication, he turned and walked out the door, his pals right on his butt.

Peters looked behind him at his team and didn't say a word. Maybe he couldn't.

Swannie finally put his hand on Peters' shoulder. "See, Frank? I told you. Not *every*body hates you."

CHAPTER SEVENTEEN

In Swannie's first year with the team, the Mavericks continued on their roll. They set records not only in Portland, but in just about every venue they visited. People came out to cheer them or boo them. In either case, the Mavs were proving to be more than just a fad. Their style may have seemed a bit salesmanshipy, or unorthodox, but, however they were doing it, they were winning baseball games.

One of their attractions was former big-league pitcher, Jim Bouton. Bouton had been persuaded by Bing to come out of retirement and try a comeback with the Mavericks in '75. Some may remember Bouton as the former Major Leaguer who described his adventures in the bigs in a book called *'Ball Four'*. Bowie Kuhn, Major League Baseball's commissioner at the time, said the book was detrimental to baseball. The commissioner wasn't alone. Other players, coaches, and officials felt that Bouton had broken an unwritten rule about telling family secrets. The book could have been called an expose, because Bouton not only described the highlights he witnessed, but the shadier side of baseball as well. Petty jealousies among the players. Obscene jokes. Drunken parties, womanizing. And the routine drug use, including by Bouton himself. In other words, Jim Bouton was the perfect Maverick.

And, with Bouton on the mound and Swannie behind the plate, the baseball term 'battery' took on a whole new implication.

(photo: Inside Sports/Shelden Sunness)

The battery of Swannie and Jim Bouton

On several occasions, the Mavericks winning ways, or perhaps their notoriety, pushed their popularity past local media and into the national spotlight. *Sports Illustrated* had a short story on them. Bouton appeared on The Johnny Carson Show and NBC Television sent Joe Garagiola to Portland to do a feature on the Mavericks.

Up until the day Garagiola met the Mavericks, he had never taken more than one day on location to conduct interviews or gather material for his show. But when he caught up with the Mavericks and their fans, he spent an extra day filming, saying, "This whole scene with Mavericks' baseball is much bigger and better than I imagined. They're really having some fun out here in Portland."

Garagiola interviewed Swannie and asked him how it felt to be a left-handed catcher.

Swannie said, "It's a lot like catching right-handed, only you do it left-handed."

Yogi Berra would have understood. (Side note: Yogi and Garagiola grew up in the same neighborhood in St. Louis, Mo. Although Garagiola made it to the Major Leagues four months ahead of Yogi, Garagiola said, "Not only am I *not* the best catcher in baseball, I'm not even the best catcher on my street!")

Before becoming a baseball announcer and TV host, Garagiola had spent nine years in the Major Leagues as a catcher for the St. Louis Cardinals, Pittsburgh Pirates, New York Giants, and the Chicago Cubs. He was considered as an adequate catcher as well as a hitter. His career batting average was .257, which would probably work well today but considered somewhat weak at the time. Towards the end of his career, Garagiola was playing for the Cubs, but hoping to pick up a radio gig in St. Louis after he retired from baseball.

In April of 1954 he was called to testify in a United States Senate subcommittee on monopoly practices by Major League Baseball. The committee chairman had sponsored a bill prohibiting corporate ownership and was targeting the St. Louis Cardinals. When the chairman, Senator Edwin Johnson, suggested the Cards were 'tampering' by trying to lure Garagiola away from the Cubs, Garagiola said, "Senator, how do you tamper for a .250 hitter?"

It was Garagiola's self-deprecating humor and his stories of being a baseball under-achiever that helped him launch, and keep, his career as a TV broadcaster for thirty-five years.

CHAPTER EIGHTEEN

Most of the trouble that the Mavericks got into, on or off the field, they did as a team. If one of them got knocked down, a teammate was there to help him up and even the score. They had each other's back. There was one exception on the Mavs, however, and he was the self-proclaimed star of the show, Reggie Thomas.

Not that Thomas didn't get into trouble, he did, but most of the time it was with a member of his own team, or most likely, whomever was the manager at the time. It seems like many teams of any sports has had a similar situation. They have player that is really a gifted athlete, usually faster than the other players, makes more money than most, and gets more press. But sometimes they come with a price. They're not locker-room friendly.

Granted, Thomas' role as a prima donna worked for Bing and Peters. They didn't mind fans in other towns hating the Mavericks. And if they wanted to focus on a certain player, it was all the more incentive for fans to come to the ballpark. The gates were usually good wherever the Mavs played. As mentioned earlier, the Mavericks did a lot of promoting in their red bus coming through small towns, loudspeaker blaring, challenging people to 'come see the game tonight!' Of course, when the people did look to see where the noise was coming from, they mostly likely saw bare asses mooning them through windows on the bus. Those darn ol' Mavericks. What's not to love?

Reggie did have a couple of friends on the team, and he didn't draw boos in quite the manner of an Alex Rodriguez or an Albert Belle, but Mr. Thomas did have a temper. He had a love-hate relationship with manager Peters and sometimes the hate part would erupt. One such example was when Frank Peters benched him for not helping to pull the tarpaulin on the field during a rain delay (The Mavericks couldn't afford a grounds crew at the time so they counted on the players to chip in).

Even though Reggie Thomas might not have been the smartest mouse in the micro-wave, he did know that scouts from the Major League often attended Mavericks games. And, Thomas knew if he's riding the bench, ain't nobody gonna be looking his way. He confronted Peters about not being in the lineup and a scuffle ensued. Peters took one in the mouth before Thomas grabbed a shovel and threaten further damage. Several Mavericks, including Kurt Russell, broke up the skirmish.

When the game was finally about to start, Peters met with the umpires with the lineup card in one hand and a handkerchief in the other, stemming the flow of blood from his mouth. Thomas didn't start the game, but played later, drawing a walk, hitting a single, and stealing two bases.

Because Thomas had helped win the game, Peters and Thomas went back to the lovey-dovey side of their relationship. Unfortunately, it didn't last.

The next incident between the two happened when the team was mired in a losing streak. Peters, in his unconventional wisdom, decided to shake things up by drawing the starting lineup out of a hat. When Thomas' name wasn't drawn, he naturally made a fuss and yelled obscenities at his field boss. This time Peters suspended him until further notice and Thomas stormed off.

Peters was sitting with Bing in the dugout just before the game started when Mavericks pitcher, Jim Emery walked up and pointed to Peters, "Reggie has a gun and he said he's gonna shoot you."

Peters looked at Bing and said, "I guess when you get suspended from the Mavericks it's the last stop at the OK Corral. If he's goin' out, it looks like he wants to take me with him."

This didn't sit well with Bing. "Wait a minute. I get top billing here! If he's gonna shoot somebody, he better shoot me first! He can shoot you second!"

Peters didn't know if Bing was kidding or not but he didn't wait around to find out. There was a small bathroom at the end of the dugout and Peters ran in and locked the door. He sat there wondering if Bing would really take the first bullet. Peters realized he still had the lineup card with him, so, he did the only thing he could think of to do in that situation; he wrote Thomas' name on it and slid it under the door. He also vowed to never try to discipline Thomas again.

Sadly, for all parties involved, Thomas would blow out a knee that season and never play again. He mysteriously died in July of 1980 and was rumored to have been an FBI informant. Frank Peters was called to testify in an investigation but never learned the outcome.

CHAPTER NINETEEN

If the people that asked Peters to testify as a credible witness were aware of some of his antics on the playing field, they might not have been so keen on seeing him raise his right hand to tell the truth and nothing but the truth.

One example of Peters' off-the-wall behavior came during the top of the fourth inning of a doubleheader against the Single A Seattle Rainiers. The game was being played in Sicks Stadium, which later housed the Seattle Pilots in their one and only year in the Majors. The Rainiers were leading, 3-1 with one out. Swannie was behind the plate and already agitated with of some of the calls that were going against his team.

With the count 3-2 on the batter, the umpire called ball four on what appeared to be strike three. Peters was out of the dugout and in the ump's face before the hitter had even tossed his bat aside. The umpire turned away from Peters, pointed to first, and loudly said, "Take your base."

Whoa! Wrong thing to say.

Peters immediately took off for first base. Within seconds the Mavs' manager had straddled the bag and pulled it up out of the ground. Umpires quickly converged on the scene to try to talk Peters down off the ledge, but he wasn't having any of it. With first base tucked under his arm, Peters strode defiantly down and through the dugout and into his clubhouse office where he slammed and locked the door. Players followed, pleading with him to calm down and give up the base. "C'mon, Frank, we can't play without it, we don't have any extra bases!"

Meanwhile, the umpiring crew had a pow-wow on the field and decided if Peters didn't return first base forthwith, the Mavs would have to forfeit the first game of the doubleheader.

Peters may have figured it was another way to motivate his team, or they were going to lose anyway, so he stayed where he was until ten minutes past forthwith. When the forfeit had been officially announced, Peters finally emerged with the goods, the base was returned to its proper position, and the second game of the doubleheader got underway. However, it didn't take long to notice that the bag had been slightly altered in appearance. It had been signed by all of the Mavericks and Todd Field, their batboy.

The jury is still out whether Frank Peters will get credit as the only person to ever steal first base.

Further evidence of Peters' stability came during a road trip to Eugene, Oregon. The Mavs and Emeralds were locked in 1-1 tie in the bottom of the seventh inning. Despite the low score there had been lots of action and great defensive plays from both teams. If you were a player, it was fun game to be in. As a fan, it was a great game to watch. You knew you would talk about this one later.

With one out and a runner on third, the Em's batter lifted a fly ball to shallow center.

The runner went back to third and waited for the center fielder to make the catch and then took off for home. The Mavs center fielder had a decent arm and had made the catch while on the run. Every beating heart at the ballpark knew it was going to be a close play at home.

Swannie tossed his mask out of the way, set up to block the plate and waited for the throw. The throw beat the runner by a tick and Swannie laid the tag on him. Swannie exuberantly jumped up and pumped his fist at his center fielder before jogging off the field toward the dugout. However, there was a problem; the ump made a delayed call of 'safe'. When Swannie realized what was going on, he was incensed and ran back toward the ump, flapping his arms and screaming his lungs out (Think George Brett with the KC Royals when he hit a home run against the NY Yankees, but was called out for using too much pine tar on his bat). As Swannie continued his rant, the fans started booing and launched a few beer bottles near home plate. Peters rushed to the scene for a couple of reasons; first, he wanted to express his opinion on the call at home, and second, he was short a catcher and he couldn't afford to have Swannie booted. He immediately got between Swannie and the ump, but the ump seemed bent on defending his call and continued pointing at home plate and arguing with Swannie.

Peters knew his catcher wasn't going to back down and wasn't long for the game if the umpire's wrath didn't get diverted. So, without a word, Peters did what any abnormal manager would do in the situation; he began taking off his clothes.

First his hat went into the air, then he tore off his jersey and flung it on home plate.

Swannie and the ump were still going at it, so Peters continued his strip tease. He kicked off his cleats and tore off his under shirt. But it wasn't until he started to drop trow, that he finally got the umpire's attention. Even Swannie was startled and backed away.

The crowd had really gotten into it and more missiles and insults were being hurled, but now they were being directed toward Peters. The umpire soon forgot about Swannie and started to get in Peters' face, but at the last-minute thought better of it. No sense in getting too close to a crazy guy. The umpire stood back, pointed at Peters and loudly yelled, "Yer outta here!"

Peters calmly stopped what he was doing, picked up his hat and started walking off the field in his stocking feet. Ignoring the insults and incoming projectiles, Peters stopped just short of the dugout, doffed his cap to the crowd, did a quick bump and grind, and then disappeared into the dugout.

The crowd went crazy but the show, however, was far from over. Bing Russell, never one to pass up an audience that was already warmed up, came out of the stands and entered the fray. He got right up in the ump's face and started arguing his call, pantomiming Swannie's tag at the plate, indicating that the runner was clearly out.

When the ump turned to walk away, Bing jumped in front of him, still jawing. The ump probably could've handled the verbiage, but when Bing added flying spittle to the dialogue, the ump flared up and loudly tossed the Mavericks' owner.

As Bing marched off the field he shouted at his batboy, Todd Field, to go pick up the rest of Peters' clothes. Todd immediately ran out to home plate and started gathering clothing. When he thought he had it all, he started off the field. He didn't get far when the ump yelled at him. The ump picked up a shoe that Todd had overlooked and threw it at him. When Todd reached to catch it, he accidentally dropped the bundle of clothes he was carrying. The umpire thought this was funny and said something like, 'nice catch'.

Todd stood stock still for a moment, his face turning red. Then he picked up the clothes again, but instead of going off the field with them, he walked over to the ump and dumped them at his feet. "Here, asshole." Then Todd turned and walked off the field.

Bing met him at the dugout with open arms.

(photo: Sue Swanson)

Kurt Russell and other Mavericks look on as Swannie prepares to carve

(photo: Seattle P-I, Aug 4, 1985)

Mavericks, left to right: Mike Holtman, Kurt Russell, Eddie Cervanties, Terry Lee, Swannie, Buster Attenberry

CHAPTER TWENTY

Meanwhile, the Mavs went 42-35 that year and finished first in the newly aligned North Division. In the three years that they had been in business, they had yet to finish worse than second. They hadn't advanced past the division play-offs to the Championship series yet, but the way they were playing, it was only a matter of time.

They were also getting a lot of people's attention, in and out of baseball, including a singer by the name of Elvis Presley.

Not many people thought of Elvis as much of a sports fan, but in 1953, when he was in high school at Humes High in Memphis, Tennessee, Elvis tried out for the football team, but didn't make the cut. He was a little awkward and shy, and known more as a mama's boy in school. Later, in 1956, when he started to become rich and famous, he got his revenge by sponsoring a community football team that let him suit up and play. They also let him name the team and proudly displayed "EP's" on their uniforms. Take that, Humes High!

As Elvis rolled along, he took up racquetball, developed a passion for karate, and enjoyed playing touch football in the days before he blubbered up. Elvis also enjoyed watching pro football and had several televisions installed in his game room in Graceland so he could watch different games at once.

Baseball might not have been Elvis's favorite sport but sources said he was interested in investing some money in the Mavericks, possibly to produce a movie with Bing and Kurt. Some say Elvis only wanted to get in on the action and sing the National Anthem at a Mavericks game, but others said he wanted to show people he was a good enough athlete to play on the team, ala, the EP's.

Whatever the reason, there was a problem, and that problem was Frank Peters.

Apparently either Elvis or some of his people (see Colonel Parker) weren't too thrilled about working with Frank The Flake.

One rumor had it that if Elvis *did* finagle a spot on the Mavs roster, he didn't want to be upstaged by their manager. They wanted a more mature, more professional director for Elvis.

This didn't really set too well with Bing. Like a lot of people in the entertainment business, Bing had heard about the shady side of Tom, 'I'm not a real colonel', Parker, and his penchant for quantity, not quality (see: any of Elvis's movies). But as the season rolled along, the pressure from Elvis's camp continued. Bing decided it wouldn't hurt to meet with E's peeps.

After one polite meeting, Bing said he'd wait until the '75 season was over to make his decision. When Peters brought the team in at first place that year it looked like he would keep his job. But, after the team lost in the first round of the play-offs again, the question for Bing was, *Presley or Peters. The King...or The Flake, hmmm.*

One thing that was *not* in Peters' favor was Bing's penchant for one-year contracts. Every player on the Mavericks had to try out to make the club each spring. If they were able to resume their positions, they had to renegotiate their contracts as well. Okay, there was one exception, and that was Swannie. Maybe it was because Swannie was a solid company man with many oblique talents, or maybe it was because he was a freak that epitomized the Mavericks' mystique. I mean, how many people can say they've seen a professional left-handed catcher in action?

In the end, Bing decided to let Frank Peters go. After all, Bing was dealing with the *King* here right? Plus, Elvis and company had agreed to Bing's choice of new manager, a decent man by the name of Jack Spring. Spring was a steady, no frills kinda guy, with Major League experience as a left-handed relief pitcher. He also had something else going for him-in; 1972 he had been the manager for the Walla Walla, Padres, a single-A team. On his team that year was a slick-fielding second baseman that hit .325. That second baseman was Kurt Russell.

And... and this is a big *and*, many of you might remember that in the 1962 movie, "It Happened at the World's Fair," a ten-year old Kurt acted alongside of Elvis, kicking him in the shin in one scene. Kurt wasn't too sure who Elvis was at that time and even gave him some advice when the two first met on the set. "You shouldn't let women jump on you like that, sir."

So, Bing had his son's relationship with Elvis to consider when he hired Spring.

CHAPTER TWENTY-ONE

Jack Spring was born in Spokane, Washington, a town that has never fielded a major league team of any kind but has been ranked the fifth best 'Minor League Sports Market in America' out of 239 markets. The area has also produced nearly two dozen Major League ballplayers, most recently, left-handed reliever Jeremy Affeldt who saw World Series action in 2014 with the San Francisco Giants. (Affeldt was burdened with weird injuries that included gashing his right hand while trying to separate frozen hamburger patties.)

Spring's hometown also produced athletes like Ryne Sandburg, Major League Hall of Fame baseball player, John Stockton, All-Star NBA player, and Mark Rypien, Superbowl MVP.

In his earlier years, Spring and had been a standout pitcher for Lewis and Clark High School baseball team and later played for Gonzaga and Washington State Universities.

While playing for several major league teams, Spring posted fairly good numbers as a reliever, going 12-5 with a 4.36 era.

The old saying, 'Hope springs eternal,' often applies to the start of baseball season. In June of 1976, tryouts for the Mavericks were held again at Civic Stadium in Portland.

Unfortunately, it wasn't long before Spring's hopes were anything but eternal.

In the first day of tryouts, Swannie was asked to don his gay apparel and sit behind the plate while others tried out in simulated games. No big deal Swannie thought. At least he didn't have to worry about making the team again.

During the simulation, with one out and a runner on third base, the batter hit a shallow fly ball to center. The runner tagged, put his head down, and with a, 'God-I-really-wanna-make-this-team,' effort, started toward home plate. Swannie set up to receive the throw from the outfield. The runner, who was wearing a batting helmet, arrived at the plate just as the ball got there. He dove headfirst and slammed into Swannie's left knee.

Swannie went down, cussing and grabbing the back of his knee. As he lay at the plate in intensive pain, it hit him that he might not be able to play baseball for a while. That's when he really started to swear.

In hindsight, Swannie probably should have just stepped aside on the play, but that was never part of his DNA.

Meanwhile, a herd of Mavericks gathered at home plate, some with Louisville Sluggers in their hands. As Swannie lay in agony, several Mavericks escorted the base runner to right field, where the exit was.

Later, at the Portland hospital, it was confirmed that Swannie had a torn anterior cruciate ligament (ACL) and would require surgery. He was looking at least six-month rehab. The 1976 season, the one that hadn't even started yet, was over for the Swandog. However, as most people in the hospital could attest to, his ability to swear had not been affected.

In hindsight, Swannie's injury was probably a blessing in disguise for a couple of reasons. Number one, it probably kept him from being disciplined, fined, or let go by Jack Spring. Unlike his predecessor, Frank, 'The Flake, I don't Have Any Rules' Peters, Spring was a, by-the-book kinda guy. The first thing he did was to re-establish signals and signs. Okay, that wasn't too much to ask, right? Most baseball teams with players older than eight use that method.

It was his second rule that most likely would've got Swannie in trouble. "No swearing in the dugout."

Swannie learned about the Mavericks' new rules during his first week of rehab. He hadn't been able to get to the ballpark, but he kept up with the team's status through the sports page and phone calls to his friends on the club. One of his first calls was to Terry Lee, his pal and shortstop.

"Hey, Terry. Looks like you guys are getting off to a good start, even without me or Frank, heh, heh."

"Yeah, we're doin' okay."

"So... how's the new skipper workin' out? He okay to play for?"

"I guess he's alright. We're still winning. But he does do things differently." "Yeah? Like what?"

"Well, for one thing, he doesn't allow swearing in the dugout."

"Oh, fuck you," Swannie said, disbelievingly. "Of course you can swear in a dugout. I think it's probably illegal to *not* to swear in *baseball* dugouts. You *are* shittin' me, right?"

"Nope. I'm not, ah...kidding you Swannie."

When Swannie didn't say anything, Lee asked him. "So, how are you? You gonna be able to hang out with us at any of our games this season?"

There was another long silence before Swannie finally answered. "You know, I think I might have to sit this one out."

The second reason that the Swannie's injury was a blessing in disguise was that it would steer him to that fork in the road that Yogi spoke of. The one you take when you get to it.

Six weeks into his rehab, Swannie took on a full-time job working as bartender at Peters Inn in Portland.

All though Frank Peters was no longer the manager of the Mavericks, he and Swannie continued their unique relationship that extended outside the white lines of the baseball field. Voicing his typical ideology, Peters said, "Swannie is the son that I'm lucky enough to never have had." When pressed to explain, Peters added, "Well you know, if he was a blood son there would be expectations, but this way, there's no expectations. Plus, I didn't have to discipline him as if he were my real son and living under the same roof with me. I just enjoyed Swannie for himself, as Swannie."

If Peters' words of wisdom seem mazy, remember they came from the same man that liked to say, "In every bridge, there's a steel lining."

Many of the Mavericks augmented their meager baseball salary by working for Peters, but when Swannie showed up at Peters Inn, it wasn't just to earn beer money, it was to learn the sports bar business.

Nobody had ever doubted Swannie's work ethic. It was there before he tossed his first newspaper. Instilled in him by his parents, and then nurtured further by Father O'Brien and coach Frederick.

Swannie knew better than to follow some of Peters' examples of management in baseball, but his methods in the bar business were something to pay attention to. Like surrounding yourself with smart personnel and letting them do their thing.

Besides noting margins in food and drinks, Swannie studied all the physical nuances of the place as well. Like where the TV's and tables were placed. Where the restrooms and phone booths were. How the kitchen and bar were set up. How the entries and exits worked to your benefit. He watched other employees' foot traffic patterns as they flowed around the place.

Swannie vowed to be physically ready to play ball the next season, but now he would have a business back-up plan as well. When he thought about it, something nagged him, kinda like a Deja vu moment. *Hmm...something about college. Something about a degree in... business?*

As Swannie kept plugging along at Peters Inn, the Mavericks kept winning, swearing be damned. By mid-July they held a 12-game lead in their division. But when Jack Spring went down with a fractured skull after slipping in the shower, Bing stepped in as interim manager. As the weeks went by, Bing kept his team on course for the division title but the rumors of Elvis' involvement in the team began to die off. On August 16, 1976, all rumors came to an end when Elvis died off too.

When the Mavs won their division that year, they faced the Walla Walla Padres in a three-game set that would determine who would advance to the Championship Series. The Padres took the opening game, 9-2 in Walla Walla, but the Mavs game back and won game two, 14-2. The final game of the play-offs was in Portland and was a much closer contest, but the Mavs still lost 7-6, and once again, Bing was looking for another manager.

CHAPTER TWENTY-TWO

In 1977, Bing hired Steve Collette as player/manager for the Mavericks. Collette was an easy-going guy who had attended Oregon College of Education, now called Western Oregon University. He played baseball while in college and was a good all-around athlete. As of this writing, Collette still holds various athletic records at WOU.

Unlike his predecessor, Jack Spring, Collette had no managerial experience. But then, neither did Hank Thompson, Frank Peters, or Bing Russell for that matter.

To kick off the Mavs' season, the first thing Collette did as player/manager was to swear in the dugout. Not profoundly, but enough to ease the tension on the club. Since most of the Mavs were adept at swearing anyway, their new manager's style set well with the players.

However, this lessening of lewd language was soon put to the test in a Mavs game that featured Christine Wren, the second woman to ever work professionally as an umpire in baseball.

Before we get to Wren, and her Mavs debut, we should tell you who the *first* woman was to work as a professional umpire. Her name was Bernice Gera, who was in her thirty's when she enrolled in a six-week training program at an umpiring school in Florida. Since umpiring had always been considered a man's job, the school had no facilities for women. Gera, who was from Pennsylvania, had to spend extra money to stay in a motel during the program. According to several reports she excelled in her training, yet when she sought work, she was rejected by the National Association of Baseball Leagues. The NABL claimed she didn't meet the physical requirements needed for the job. (You'd think they could've let her know that a little bit earlier...?)

Apparently, the NABL didn't know that you should never piss off a woman named Bernice. Gera took the NABL to court and battled them for five years before she finally won a discrimination suit against them.

So it was, on June 23, 1972, Gera gained National attention by being the first woman to umpire a professional baseball game. It was Minor League Class A doubleheader between the Auburn Twins and the Geneva Senators.

In the fourth inning of the game, an Auburn batter tried to stretch a single into a double. Wren initially called him safe at second but realized she had made the wrong call and quickly reversed it and called him out. The Auburn manger stormed out of the dugout to protest, telling Gera that her first mistake was putting on an umpire's uniform, her second mistake was blowing the call. He became so belligerent that Gera eventually ejected him. When he didn't go quietly, Gera looked around for help from the other umps. She was greatly disappointed when they turned and walked away, letting her fend for herself.

Her disappointment was so intense that instead of being behind the plate for the next game of the doubleheader, she walked off the field and away from her dream.

"I beat them in the courts, but I can't beat them on the field," she later said.

Gera did stay in baseball however and worked for the New York Mets in their public relations department for five years before retiring to Florida. She died of cancer in 1992 at the age of 61. Because of the doors she opened for both men and women who are discriminated against because of arbitrary restrictions, her photograph, pink whisk broom, and uniform are on display in the Hall of Fame in Cooperstown, New York.

Now, back to Christine Wren who was well aware of Gera's struggle and gender discrimination but was just as determined to make it as an umpire as Gera was. In the early 70's, Wren attended the Bill Kinnamon Specialized Umpire Training Course in Southern California. After graduation Wren took a number of different jobs to pay the rent but she continued to attend as many baseball games and other sporting events as she could, always studying the officiating.

In the mid-seventies, Wren was working in an auto-body shop when the phone rang.

Wren's co-worker took the call, listened for a few seconds, and then hung up. "Who was that? Wren asked. "A prank call," her co-worker said. "Some guy saying he was Peter O'Malley. Looking for you."

Wren hesitated a second and then said, "Yeah, right. Like the owner of the Dodgers is gonna call me. Ha."

A few minutes later, the phone rang again, but this time Wren answered. It was the same guy saying he was Peter O'Malley wanting to talk to a Ms. Christine Wren. Wren had heard and seen O'Malley on television enough to recognize his voice. It *was* him! He was calling to ask her if she would like to umpire an exhibition game between the Dodgers and the University of Southern California at Dodger Stadium!

Wren quickly accepted the offer which turned out to be one of the biggest thrills of her life. She said of the experience, "Walking out in front of fifty-thousand fans in Dodger Stadium, if that doesn't give you chills, then nothing will. I will remember that for the rest of my life." It was also the game that got her noticed and hired to work in Single-A league the following year.

When Wren did make her debut at a Mavericks game at Civic Stadium in Portland, there were probably forty-nine thousand less fans then there had been at Dodger Stadium, but it would be a game she would remember for the rest of her life as well.

It was a home game for the Mavs against the Eugene Emeralds. The battery for the Mavericks that day was Bouton and Swannie. Wren called 'play ball' and the Mavs took the field.

The Em's lead-off batter swung on the first pitch and flied out to centerfield. The next batter hit Bouton's first pitch to right field for a single. Wren hadn't had to call a ball or a strike yet. Then the fun began.

Because Bouton was primarily a knuckleball pitcher at that point in his career, he basically threw the butterfly ball ninety percent of the time. And if you've ever had the privilege, or misfortune to *try* to catch a knuckleball, the only thing you know for sure is, you don't know for sure where the damn thing is going. Most of the time, the pitcher doesn't even know.

Anyway, the next batter took the first two pitches which Wren called balls. Swannie saw them differently but didn't say anything. *Maybe Wren has never seen a knuckleball thrown by a former Major League pitcher?*

With the count at 2-0, the batter took another pitch that eventually floated in, belt high, right across the plate. "Ball," Wren said again.

Swannie immediately stood and threw his hands up in disgust, but quickly made it look like he was calling time-out. He jogged out to the mound to have a word with Bouton. Apparently Swannie wasn't concerned with people reading his lips because he didn't even cover his mouth with his glove when he reached the mound. The word he was having with Bouton rhymed with 'suck' and he screamed it quite clearly.

Bouton, being the seasoned professional that he was, calmed his catcher down, and after a few moments Swannie trotted back to his position behind home plate. With the count now at 3-0, Bouton turned another knuckleball loose that eventually danced its way right across the middle of the plate, just below the letters. "Ball!" cried Wren.

Swannie caught the ball but didn't move. He just stayed in his crouch, frozen in position and staring straight ahead. He let a few seconds pass and then, without looking back at Wren, he calmly said, "Your strike zone must be as big as your dick."

Wren may not have much experience ejecting players or managers, but she reacted just like a pro when she immediately gave Swannie the heave-oh. "You're outta here!"

Collette immediately charged out of the dugout and got right in Wren's face. "Whadda ya doin'? Why you throwin' him out? What'd he do?!"

"Ask him." Wren said, and turned her back and started walking away, acting like she was looking at her count clicker in her right hand.

Collette looked at Swannie. "What'd you do?"

"Nothin'. I just told her that her strike zone must be as big as her dick."

Collette thought Swannie was just kidding so he went after Wren. When Wren turned around, Collette said to her, "I gotta right to know what my player did or said that got him tossed. He won't tell me. So, what was it? What'd he say'?"

Wren took a breath, got in Collette's face and repeated what Swannie had said, word for word.

Collette was suddenly speechless and his face reddened. He stared at Wren until he finally gurgled something that sounded like Ralph Cramden from the Honeymooners, 'ha-ma-na, ha-ma-na'.

Swannie finally stepped in and came to his manager's rescue by leading him by the arm toward the dugout as if he was the one being tossed. Someone from the dugout yelled to Wren, "Welcome to baseball lady...and the wonderful world of weirdness!"

Not long after that incident, Wren was scheduled to work another Mavericks game. She was behind the plate again, calling balls and strikes for the same battery of Bouton and Swanson. When Swannie realized who was umpiring that day, he put his jersey on backwards in hopes Wren wouldn't notice his name. When he crouched in front of Wren for the first pitch, she called him on it. "Isn't *your name* supposed to be on the back of your uniform?"

"Oh, yes ma'am. It is. Maverick. That's my real name." "I thought so," Wren said. "Play ball!"

(photo: National Baseball Hall of Fame)

Christine Wren in uniform

(photo: National Baseball Hall of Fame)

Wren in her van studying the rules of baseball

CHAPTER TWENTY-THREE

With Steve Collette at the helm, Swannie's duties as utility man were pleasantly downsized. As a player, Collette handled himself very well in the field and at the plate. He was also a good manager, made the right moves at the right time and was well liked by his players. Thus, he didn't require a bodyguard.

However, as the season rolled along, some of the Mavericks' mannerisms subtly rubbed off on Collette. In other words, he wasn't above some hi-jinx of his own.

One such opportunity came when the Mavs traveled to Salem, Oregon, to play a doubleheader against the Salem Senators. After taking both games, the team checked into a hotel. It was late Sunday night, but a couple of the Mavs, namely Eddie Cervantes and Swannie, were feeling frisky. They were wondering if it was possible to find a little girly action at such an hour.

Just before they stepped out of the hotel, they bumped into Collette in the lobby.

They both knew that Collette was from Salem, so they asked him for a recommendation. "Hey Steve. Anything shaking' around here?"

Collette thought for a moment. He looked at his watch and said, "I think I know just the place. It's called Tara's Pub. It's within walking distance." After giving them directions, Collette added. "You'll probably get all the action you can handle there. Some professional, if you know what I mean?"

Cervantes and Swannie's eyes lit up. "Cool frijoles, amigo! Let's went!" They took a couple of steps toward the door, before looking back at Collette "You coming with, man?"

Collette hesitated and then said, "Ah...I'll catch up. I gotta a couple of things to do here first. Go ahead, I'll see you soon."

Swannie and Cervantes walked the short distance and found the place with no problem. The building wasn't much to look at from the outside, but they were confident that their pal, Collette, knew what he was talking about.

When they stepped inside, they were even more excited. Although the lighting was very dim, they could see a dance floor that was packed with couples and they were all rockin' to the Bee Gees latest hit, "Stayin' Alive." Beyond the dance floor there was a long bar where the lighting was somewhat better and they thought they could see several women sitting on stools, chatting, smoking, drinking and laughing.

Swannie and Cervantes high-fived each other and started toward the bar, holding on to a handrail to guide them in the darkness. Just before they reached the bar, a tall brunette with long dangling, silver earrings, reached out and grabbed Swannie's arm. "C'mon, Sugar. They're playing our song. Let's get *down*!"

Swannie looked back at Cervantes, smiling. "Order me a beer, pal. I'll meet you back at the bar!"

As Swannie boogied away with his new love, Cervantes made it to the bar and pulled up a stool. There were two men working behind the bar and the one closest came over to Cervantes. He had somewhat of a pained looked on his face, but shouted over the music, "Whaddya want here?"

Cervantes thought the guy was being a little rude but figured maybe he had already put in a long shift in a loud joint.

"Two Miller draughts, please."

As the man walked away, Cervantes eye-balled a couple of women sitting at the bar. A slim redhead who looked like Lucile Ball, face paint, eyelashes and all, was smiling at her companion who could have passed for Dolly Parton, minus the bust. They seemed to be comparing fashion notes. Lucy reached up and gently touched the side of Dolly's face. Dolly turned her head slightly one way and then the other, as if to show Lucy her new hairstyle. They both burst out laughing. Dolly sucked in a long drag off of her cigarette, tilted her head back, and blew smoke straight up in the air. The two giggled some more and then Lucy held out her arm and jangled about four pounds of bracelets on her wrist for her friend to inspect.

They must have felt Cervantes staring at them because they both suddenly stopped what they were doing and looked straight at him. Lucy smirked. Dolly blew him a kiss.

Boom! It finally hit him. Cervantes looked around him. He looked at the other couples. He looked out at the dance floor. The music had just stopped and people were making their way back to their tables and to the bar.

"What's the matter, boy?" the bartender said as he set two beers down on the bar. "Just figuring things out are ya?"

Cervantes looked at the bartender. Then he looked at the two beers. He didn't know what to do. Shit, spit, or...split? He could feel Lucy and Dolly looking at him.

About that time, Swannie walked up to the bar next to Cervantes He was sweating and smiling. He leaned over with his elbows against the bar and said to Cervantes, "Hey, buddy! You gotta get your ass out on the dance floor, man. Some of these babes can really boogie!"

Cervantes just looked at his pal but said nothing. Then Swannie looked around. He looked at the bartender. Then he looked at Dolly and Lucy. Nobody was saying anything. "What? What's the matter?" Swannie asked.

Finally, the bartender enlightened Swannie. "You know that *babe* you were dancing with?"

"You mean, Francis?" "No. I mean Frank."

"Frank? Who the fuck is Frank?" "Frank's the babe behind you."

Swannie turned around. Francis, aka Frank, smiled and grabbed Swannie's butt. "You're mine, Sugar Pie."

Swannie's synapses fired and he launched a left hook before his brain told him not to.

The punch caught Frankie flush on the jaw, snapping his head back. His wig flew off and he went down like a sack of Joe Fraziers.

Lucy screamed and Dolly jumped off of his stool and went after Swannie. Cervantes went after Dolly. And just like that, the place went up for grabs.

In the dim light, some patrons pushed to get closer to the action while the rest of them turned to flee, which just escalated the situation. Sidebar arguments broke out and more punches thrown. Chairs and tables were crunching and glass was breaking. Lots of yelling and screaming.

Finally, the house lights came on, and the scene looked like a Halloween party gone bad.

A couple of men were holding Swannie down on the floor while Cervantes was in the process of flipping a body off of his back. The bartender kept yelling for everybody to stop what they were doing. Finally, two cops came hustling in and the place quieted down. People got up off of the floor and began dusting themselves off.

"He started it", someone yelled and pointed out Swannie. "Him and his buddy over there."

One of the cops told everybody to shut up and asked the bartender. "What's going on here, same ol' shit?"

"That's right, officer," the bartender said as he made his way over to the cops. "These two guys comin' in here, startin' trouble. We're gettin' real tired of it."

The cop frowned and said, "I bet you are. But, if it's any consolation, my partner and I are getting tired of it too. It's not like your place is job security for us or anything, you know?"

The cop waved Swannie and Cervantes toward him. "Okay, you two. Let's go." Swannie had the audacity to ask where.

It was three in the morning when Bing showed up at the Salem Police station and bailed his players out of jail.

The first thing Swannie asked his boss after being released was, "Are we off the team?"

Bing tilted his head and asked, "Either of you have any broken bones that would keep you from playing?"

Swannie and Cervantes looked each other as if to inspect the other guy for damages.

They both shook their heads. "No. We're good." Cervantes answered.

Bing said, "The police chief told me that all the other, ah, participants, were able to walk away, so unless the owner of the club wants to press charges, you guys are still playing. I'll have to make it right to the owner of course, you know, pay for the damages and all."

Bing seemed to be taking everything quite well, and before Swannie or Cervantes could say anything more, Bing said, "Actually, we may able to use this little incident to our advantage. The publicity and all."

Swannie and Cervantes looked at each again, completely dumbfounded this time. Bing explained. "This story is bound to make the newspapers (*The Oregon Statesman,* Tuesday, August 9, 1977), so here's what I'm thinkin'; We publicly invite the owner and patrons of Tara's Pub to be our special guests at one of our up-coming home games. We make sure the right newspapers get this of course, and then we promote the game as ten-cent beer night! Should be wild. Whaddya think?"

Swannie answered for both of them. "We think you're the best boss a guy could ever have!"

A week later, the Mavericks held their ten-cent beer night in a home game against Salem. And because nothing connected to the Mavericks should surprise anyone, at least twenty of the gals/guys from Tara's Pub showed up in their finest attire for the event.

And to further prove that all was forgiven, the group even carried a sign that read, "We love the Mavericks and Swannie! He can really hit!" The Mavericks' mystique had survived another one.

CHAPTER TWENTY-FOUR

As mentioned earlier, Swannie's function as the team's utility man was not limited by normal definitions. Even after a bit of a lay-off as utility man, the Swandog still had an uncanny ability to morph into whatever the situation called for. He learned early on that the more positions he could play for the team, the more secure his job would be.

Actually, this type of thinking could be applied in many job situations in today's market as well. An example might be found at a television or radio station where, hypothetically speaking, there were some lay-offs pending. Let's say you were the one that could not only handle a microphone but could double as a plumber when the station's toilet plugged up? Or, you could put on a tool-belt and remodel the office? Paint the place? Mow the boss's lawn?

Being in charge of checking the team into hotels was just another arrow in Swannie's quiver. As mundane as it sounds, the job could at times require patience and diplomacy. Take for instance the time the Mavs had traveled north for a game with the Bellingham Mariners. The Mavs had just arrived in town and was unloading their bus while Swannie was inside at the registration desk taking care of business.

A couple in their eighties owned and managed the place and the husband was at the front desk moving about as fast as the grandfather clock that was behind him. As the players rolled into the lobby, Swannie handed out room keys to the players. One of the first players to get a key was Mavs pitcher Phil Marino.

Two minutes after Marino checked into his room on the second floor, he was back in the lobby. "Hey! The TV's not working in my room. What's goin' on?" Marino was obsessed with local news channels so he could check the weather forecasts for game time conditions.

The husband was bent over the desk slowly filling out the paperwork and didn't look up. Marino yelled at him again. This time the old man answered but still didn't look up, "I'll look at it when I'm finished here, sir."

Marino looked at Swannie, motioned for him to kick the old fart in the butt, and then went back upstairs to his room.

Twenty minutes later, Swannie was still at the desk trying to get players checked in. By now the husband had called for his wife to come out and help him but she had yet to show.

Marino came out again and yelled down to the old man. "Hey, mister! What the hell do I have to do to get my goddamn television to work!?"

The manager stopped writing and slowly took off his glasses. He looked up at Marino and enunciated clearly, "I-will-look-at-the-problem...when-I-have-time...sir." Then just as slowly, he replaced his glasses and began writing in his ledger again.

This sent Marino through the roof. "Goddamn it! You'll probably die before the TV comes on!"

Just as Marino was finishing his broadside, the man's wife came around the corner.

She threw her hand over her mouth and hurried to her husband.

Swannie quickly went into damage control by laughing it off. "Oh, don't you guys pay any attention to him. He's just kidding. Phil does that to everyone. In fact, he's writing a book about the kind of reaction he gets from people. He's actually a really nice guy."

The woman wasn't buying it and told her husband he should call the police and have the team thrown out. Swannie continued his song and dance long enough to convince the woman to help her husband. "You know, the sooner we get checked in, the sooner you won't hear from us again, I promise."

Without another word the woman took over from her husband and started dealing keys to Swannie. Swannie was wise enough to keep his mouth shut until she finished. When he had everybody checked in, Swannie headed for Marino's room. His plan was to either trade rooms with Marino, or, fix the television his own bad self. After all, he was a professional utility man. Marino had cooled off somewhat and had already put most of his gear away. He contritely agreed to let Swannie tinker with the set. "If you get that fucker to come on, I'm *really* gonna feel like an ass."

After about twenty minutes of fiddling with the Sylvania, they both agreed it was beyond their expertise. It wasn't long after that that they heard a siren in the distance.

The wailing grew louder until it reached the hotel and then it quickly died away.

Swannie and Marino stepped out of the room and walked down the hallway until they were looking down at the reception desk. They watched as a couple of medics hustled a gurney around the desk and into the back room. Swannie and Marino looked at each other with their mouths open.

Fifteen quiet minutes passed before the gurney slowly came back out again with the old man's body on it. The lady followed, sobbing into her handkerchief. A crowd had gathered by this time, but when she looked up and saw Marino and Swannie she pointed at them and screamed, "You killed him! You killed my husband! Get out of here! All of you. Get out of here! Now!"

Nobody on the Mavericks had to be told what to do next. Within twenty minutes they were all packed and back aboard the bus, looking for another place to stay. Marino sat by himself in the front of the bus in silence. Nobody was saying, but they were all thinking the same thing; *be careful of what you wish for.*

CHAPTER TWENTY-FIVE

As mentioned earlier, Mavericks players came from far and wide. Pitcher Rob Nelson is a case in point. Nelson was a left-handed pitcher who had had success in college pitching for Cornell University where he graduated with a degree in philosophy. After college, Nelson chased his dream of pitching professionally. He tried out wherever he could and in whatever league would have him. His love for baseball was so great that he eventually wound up pitching in South Africa. After a game one day, Nelson happened to come across a copy of the *Sporting News* and noticed an article about Bing Russell's project in Single A ball. Nelson caught the next flight out of Africa and made connections to Portland, Oregon.

Players trying to make the Mavericks did come from all over, but Nelson held the distinction of having come the farthest. Needless to say, he was the only walk-on from Africa-- or from Cornell University for that matter.

Nelson had some success pitching for the Mavs but at times would struggle. One day in a game with Swannie behind the plate, the first seven batters that Nelson faced all blasted his first pitch for a base hit. The score was 4-0 and the bases were loaded before Steve Collette called time out. On the way to the mound, Collette asked Swannie what kind of pitches Nelson was throwing. Swannie said, "I don't know. I haven't caught one yet."

Nelson never made it to the big leagues, but he did make it big while he was with the Mavericks. One evening before a game in 1977, Nelson, Bouton, and Swannie were gathered in the bullpen when the question came up about where the term 'bullpen' came from. Nelson said he thought it came from back in 1910 when ads for Bull Durham tobacco were plastered on walls in every ballpark in the country. Pitchers would warm up in the shade of these signs. That may, or may not, be the correct origin of the term bullpen, but it works nicely here, so we'll go with that one.

Anyway, while the trio stood there jawing, they noticed some of the younger players trying to spit chewing tobacco on each other's white shoes.

"That's disgusting," Nelson said.

"What's disgusting?" asked Bouton. "That they're shitty spitters, or that they chew tobacco?"

"Both." said Nelson. "They're trying to look like big leaguers but they suck at it."

Ironically, when Nelson was a kid, his idol was Nellie Fox who always played with a humongous wad of chewing tobacco embedded in his cheek. Growing up, Nelson would try to emulate his hero but he would get sick when he used tobacco. So, like a lot of other players, Nelson resorted to cramming Bazooka Bubble Gum in his mouth, but the look just wasn't the same.

Then on that day in the dugout, Nelson told Bouton, "I always thought if you could make some sorta shredded bubblegum, you could look cool and not puke."

Bouton, who was 38 at the time, looked at Nelson with $$$ in his eyes. "My friend, I think you might have something there. I bet we could sell that idea!"

The more they talked about it, the more they thought it was a good idea. Finally, they shook hands on it and just like that, they became partners. They did some quick figuring and looked around for some start-up money. They asked Swannie if he wanted to invest five thousand in the project. Swannie asked, "Five thousand...what? *Dollars*? Are you shittin' me?"

Even though Swannie wasn't sold on the idea, Nelson and Bouton went ahead with it.

They found a recipe on how to make chewing gum and convinced batboy, Todd Field, that they would cut him in on the deal if he would help slice the product into strips in his mother's kitchen. It helped that Nelson was dating Todd's sister at the time.

After coloring their product brown to resemble tobacco, they came up with a pouch that also looked like the real deal. Once they had some samples ready, they pitched it to several sponsors, and ironically, it was Amurol Products, a subsidiary of the chewing gum magnate, William Wrigley, Jr, who eventually bought it.

Amurol Products introduced Big League Shew-BLC-in 1980 and within a year they had sold $18 million worth of product! Swannie's reaction was, "Eighteen million...what? *Dollars*? Are you shittin' me?"

In 1982, the entire franchise of the Chicago Cubs sold for only slightly more, at $20 million.

Of course, one of the reasons that BLC was, and is, successful, it provided young kids and players an alternative to chewing and spitting tobacco.

The kind of paychecks that Rob Nelson received later in life enabled him to continue pitching well into his fifties in countries like Australia, England, and South Africa. He probably would have been welcome in Singapore too, where spitting is illegal.

It must also be noted that in his heyday, Joe Garagiola advocated against tobacco use and heartily endorsed Nelson's Big-League Chew when it reached the market.

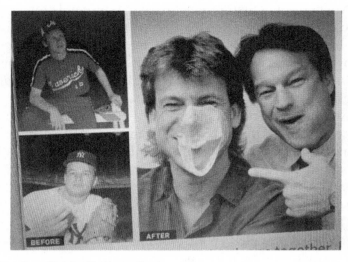

(photo: Dave Sheinin, Washington Post)

Rob Nelson with Jim Bouton blowin' away the competition

(photo: Dave Sheinin, Washington Post)

Original design of Big-League Chew

CHAPTER TWENTY-SIX

Bing and the Mavericks' way of doing things over the years had received a lot of national publicity. Along with the Garagiola special, there were mentions in *Sports Illustrated* and the *New Yorker* magazines. This attention helped to fuel the buzz and keep the turnstiles going, but even so, some of the lords in the hierarchy of baseball were not pleased. In fact, they were getting downright annoyed with Bing's antics. Lighting brooms on fire and dancing on the visitors' dugout when they might sweep a series? A dog trained to run out on the field to disrupt games as needed? A manager that steals first base? A left-handed catcher? Dime-beer night? Who did Mr. Russell think he was anyway? Fielding a team of miss-fits that didn't play by the Blue Book of Baseball? Oh, sure, they won their share of baseball games, they just weren't always polite about it.

According to one of the many unwritten rules of Major League Baseball, an Independent Class A team shouldn't be beating up on clubs that were fathered by the Los Angeles Dodgers or the Chicago Cubs.

But the one thing that always got the attention of the brass in the bigs...? $$$!!!

Money, honey! Show me the money! And the Mavs did just that. Bings' boys set the record for the highest attendance record in the Northwest League's history.

Another thing that bothered the corporate cats was that Bing Russell was making money while flipping off baseball's old-time religion. Bing kept all commercial sponsorships outside the gates of Civic Stadium. In other words, no pictures of a smiling man enjoying a Lucky Strike Cigarette or a bottle of Schlitz Beer on the outfield fences.

Finally, in 1977, the powers that be in baseball were wringing their hands in earnest. They wanted Triple AAA baseball back in Portland so they could reap the harvest Bing had planted. They wanted control again. *Hmm, what to do, what to do?*

98

Eventually, someone in the 'show' came up with a way to deal with the situation. They would simply buy Bing out. They would inform Mr. Russell that they would be taking over the Portland area again. The standard price for a Single A team at the time was five-thousand dollars, exactly what Bing had originally paid. However, since the baseball execs were such swell guys and wanted to show good faith, they agreed to offer Bing at least *five times* what he had paid for the club. Probably come in around twenty-five thousand dollars. *Alright! Yippee! Problem solved!*

When the 1977 season began winding down, Bing became aware of the rumblings from above and could feel the irony that was looming. Five years earlier he had ridden into town and herded his dream to reality. But *because* he had been so successful, he was about to be pushed aside by Major League Baseball.

He didn't share this news with anyone because the Mavs were in another pennant race and he wanted his club to stay focused. In the five years that Bing owned the Mavericks, the only thing missing was the League Championship. He wanted nothing more than to win the big one before he rode off into the sunset. But first, he had to make it to the play-offs.

In 1977, the Mavericks won their division by 22 games and advanced to the Championship Series against the Bellingham Mariners in a best of three series for the Northwest League title. The Mariners played in front of a measly home crowd of 575 'fans', but took the opener 6-2 with Bouton taking the loss. The next game was played in Portland and the Mavericks won easily, 10-1, setting up a third and deciding game at Civic Stadium for all the marbles.

The Portland's Maverick baseball team didn't know it at the time, but they were about to play the last game in the team's history.

According to the Hollywood script, the Mavs would win the game and carry Bing off the field on their shoulders. They would celebrate in the locker room for a while, and Bing would tell them how proud of them he was. He would have all the championship rings sized for the players' middle fingers. Then he would give them the news that it was the end of the ride for the Mavericks.

But, since art only imitates life, life ruled that day. In the final game going into the bottom of the ninth, Bellingham led 4-2. With one out and a runner on first and second, the Mavs' third baseman, Bobby Edwards came to the plate. A crowd of 7,805 were on their feet as Edwards worked the count to 3-2. Edwards hit a sharp ground ball to the left of the infield, but the Mariners' shortstop made a great play that started a double play to end the game.

As could be expected, it was quiet in the losers' locker room. A few guys moved to the showers while others just sat in their uniforms staring at the walls or down at their cleats. After about thirty minutes, Bing came out of his office and started handing out beers. He waited for the suds to ease the pain a little, and when the guys started feeling a little better and talking about next year, Bing called everybody together. It was time to bring the final curtain down.

The players were stunned of course, most of them knew their baseball career was over. It was a sad scene for a while, but then Bing did what he did best; he said things from his heart to the team he loved. He told them how proud he was of every man, woman, batboy, batgirl, bus driver, and dog in the Mavericks organization.

One of the last things Bing said to his players as a team was, "I'm sorry it ended this way...but that's the way the pickle squirts." And then, in true Mavericks tradition, they all proceeded to drink themselves silly...er.

CHAPTER TWENTY-SEVEN

It may have been the end of the war for the Mavericks, but it was just the beginning of Bing's battle with the Pacific Coast League. The executives of the PCL politely waited two days after the season was over to call Bing and arrange a meeting. They wanted to go over the financial details ASAP so Bing could vacate the baseball throne in Portland.

Bing, being no dummy, wasn't coming to the showdown alone. When the League had initially announced the take-over, Bing immediately hired a local lawyer, a straight shooter by the name of Jack Faustin. Faustin was also a fan of baseball and the Mavericks. Bing still knew how to pick a team.

The day of the meeting, the parties met in a downtown office, four representatives of the PCL and Bing and Faust. After coffee and Danishes, they all got down to business. The leader of the delegation for the PCL stood up smiling and declared, "We're excited about bringing Triple A baseball back to Portland and we're happy to tell you we've been given the okay to pay you twenty-six thousand dollars for the Mavericks!" His entourage smiled at Bing and nodded excitedly, as if to say; *We are not kidding. Really. That's more than five times what you paid! Can you believe that?*

Bing was all smiles himself, and turned to Faust, who smiled back at him. Then, in unison, the two stood up as if they were going to shake on the deal. When the people on the other side of the table jumped up to do the same, Bing laughed, and said, "Put a zero between the two and the six and we'll talk!"

Without another word, Bing and Faust headed for the door. The PCL'ers were stunned and didn't say anything. Just before Bing got to the door, he stopped at the table where the Danishes were and picked one up. "One for the road," he said, and then waved adios.

Nobody at the negotiations table said anything for a moment. Finally, the man in charge of the gathering asked, "He won't take twenty-six thousand? Who'n the hell does he think he is?!"

"Clem Foster," said one of the suits. "Who?"

"Clem Foster. The deputy on Bonanza, aka, Bing Russell."

Baseball and The Pacific Coast League were not about to be held up by any tin-horn independent club owner. They stood by their offer and moved to oust Bing and his Mavericks from the Portland area through the courts. But with that move they just played into Bing's hands.

Jack Faust was acutely aware of the Sherman Antitrust Act of 1890 which guarded against corporation monopolies. Of course, the baseball guys had some pretty smart cookies in their arsenal too, but maybe they could see a way around it. In 1949, AT&T had been excused from antitrust laws because the thinking then was that as a company, AT&T was vital to national security and any deregulation might interrupt service.

Perhaps MLB thought that since they were up and rolling as a business fourteen years before the Sherman act in 1876 that they too were above reproach. Grandfathered in, as it were. Could it be because they considered themselves the National Pastime, it should equate with national security? AT&T got away with it right? Well, maybe AT&T did get away with something in '49, but in 1974, they were in court against the Sherman thing again. Bing's lawyer had a professional interest in the AT&T case at the time and had monitored it closely. By 1977, the smart money was trending toward Sherman's act this time. That's when Bing told Faust to file for arbitration, saying, "What the hell. Let's put baseball on trial."

The case eventually found its way to the Oregon Supreme Court. In the fall of '77 with lawyers, owners, media and just plain folk looking on, the court made its decision. Bing Russell was granted the extra zero he was looking for and set yet another record. He was awarded the highest payout for a minor league territory in history, $206,000.00!

It was a bittersweet ending for Bing. He was able to ride back to Hollywood with gold in his saddlebags, but no ring on his middle finger. As for the other Mavericks, most of them went quietly back to whatever it was that they were doing before Bing Russell had shown them the brass ring. Todd Field would later describe the dismantling of the Mavericks, "It was like the circus left town, never to come back."

Of course, a few of the Mavericks did go on to achieve fame in other lines of work.

Pitcher Larry Colton became a writer and earned a Pulitzer Prize nomination for his efforts. Todd Field became an actor and an Academy Award nominated film maker. Kurt Russell went back to being Kurt Russell. Frank Peters ran for Governor of Oregon but lost. Peters was later busted for a romp with an underage lady and served 2 years in the Oregon State Prison. He was, however, elected captain of the prison basketball team.

Swannie? He realized his playing days were over. Wisely, he hung up his catcher's mitt and began working on the next chapter of his life.

CHAPTER TWENTY-EIGHT

In 1978, before Frank Peters ran afoul of the law, he opened another Peters Inn, but this one was located in downtown Seattle. The first person he hired to work there was Swannie who assumed the role of manager and bartender when Peters was away.

Aside from winning the first Stanley Cup for the U.S. in 1917, the city of Seattle never had the long sports tradition of a New York or a Chicago. But when the World's Fair opened in April of 1962, things became to change for Seattle. People from around the country became aware of the potential of the city in several aspects, including business and professional sports. The Seattle Opera House and The Seattle Repertory Theater both opened in 1963. And, the idea of major league franchises that had lain dormant for so long now began to percolate. Finally, in 1967, Seattle's first modern-day Major-League franchise came to town in the form of the Seattle Supersonics basketball team. The Sonics were an NBA team that was named for a contract the Boeing Company had been awarded for the Super Sonic Transport Project, or SST. That Boeing contract was later canceled, but the Supersonics name, and team, stayed.

Two years later, Major League Baseball came to town in the form of the Seattle Pilots. Although the Pilots played at Sicks Stadium, a minor league field, and lasted just one year before moving to Milwaukee, the citizens of Seattle felt they were gaining equity as a major league city on all fronts.

When the Starbucks Coffee Company opened in Seattle in 1971 everyone started talking faster and one of their favorite talking points was about building a domed multi-purpose stadium in hopes of luring an NFL team as well as another baseball team to join the fray.

The coffee must have done the trick, because in 1972 construction began on the Kingdome Stadium, a project nea downtown that had previously been voted down twice by King County taxpayers.

On August 1st, 1976, with construction on the stadium finished, the new NFL expansion team, the Seattle Seahawks, took the field for the first time in an exhibition game against the San Francisco Forty-Niners. The transformation of Seattle to a major league city was now complete. Well, not quite. There was still the opening of the first 'Underground Comedy-Club/Sports Bar' in the Northwest to go.

CHAPTER TWENTY-NINE

Frank Peters and Swannie had many fond memories from their Mavericks daze, but they had a good idea that they'd never draw another paycheck from professional baseball, so they focused their energies into the sports bar business. Swannie continued to work and pay his dues at the Peters' Inn, dreaming of the day he would flee the nest and open up his own joint somewhere.

Swannie didn't want to run too far from Peter's Inn, but at the same time he wanted to find a location far enough away that he wouldn't be in competition with his former manager. He even asked Peters' advice about looking for a place.

"There's three things you gotta know," Peters said. "First-"

"I know, location, location, location," Swannie said impatiently. "Tell me something I don't know."

Peters looked at him. "Hey! That's not bad. Location, location location...hmm...I like it...anyway, what I was gonna say was, number one; look at the history of the area, know what it used to be. Number two; look at what it's doing now and who's doing it. Number three, look at what it could be."

Swannie thought that the 'location' thing was easier to remember, but he also knew he would consider what Peters was saying.

The obvious choice for a sports bar would seem to be to get as close to where the sports are. Kinda like Dillinger's reasoning for robbing banks; "Because that's where they keep the money."

But to be close to the new Kingdome Stadium, you would also be close to Pioneer Square, the area known as the birthplace of 'modern' Seattle (not to be confused with 'non-modern' Seattle). Once a prosperous area, Pioneer Square had long ago fallen on hard times.

A restoration effort began in the sixties to clean up the area but homeless people, panhandlers, drugs and crime, were still very much a part of the experience in the area.

Still, it was an area that Swannie was interested in. Rents were cheap and a new professional sports venue close.

One day, Swannie took off early from work and walked down to Pioneer Square and literally started window shopping. When he noticed a 'for-lease' sign in one of the windows, he shaded his eyes and looked into the building. The room was vacant except for a couple of chairs and empty cardboard boxes. Without too much imagination Swannie visualized a sports bar set-up. He saw himself behind the bar serving a packed house. He saw pretty waitresses scurrying around with drink laden trays. He saw people laughing and heard music playing.

He stepped back, looked at the three-story building and sized up the situation. The outside of the structure wasn't anything special, at ground level there were three large windows and a single-entry door. The stories above had small windows that looked like they'd never been opened. Rather typical architecture for the area, but again Swannie consulted his imagination and could see how some personal touches could help with curb appeal.

The one big thing that he didn't have to imagine was the street sign just east of where he stood; Second and Main, well within walking distance of the new Kingdome Stadium that could hold fifty-thousand thirsty fans.

Then an almost spiritual feeling about the area settled over him. Some mojo working here? Maybe it had something to do with Pioneer Square not being a square at all but more of a triangle. Whatever was going on, he was pretty sure he had found his spot.

He found a pay phone and called Mr. Masin immediately. Masin offered to show him the place but was tied up at the moment. Swannie asked a couple of questions about the lease and then agreed to meet with Masin in two days.

After he got off the phone Swannie was excited and wanted to tell Peters about his find, but then the thought crossed his mind that he might be asking Peters for a loan to swing the deal. He knew his boss would ask if he had done his research.

With two days to kill, Swannie went to the library and began his due diligence.

He hadn't planned on spending too much time on the research, just enough to prove to Peters that he'd done it. However, one of the first things Swannie learned was that he couldn't bring alcoholic beverages into the library. Still, he pushed on...and surprisingly became absorbed in what he read.

CHAPTER THIRTY

In 1852, early settlers landed at Alki Point in the Pacific Northwest which is across the bay from what is now Seattle. Within a short period of time these settlers made friends with the Duwamish and Suquamish Indian tribes that lived east of them, across the bay. After sharing meals, trading goods, and smoking some of their good stuff, the settlers realized that the Indians lived in a better neighborhood than they did.

So, being good Americans, the settlers pulled up stakes, moved across the bay and set up shop in a nice area that the Chief Si'ahl of the Suquamish had recommended. There was a deeper harbor there than what Alki offered, and it was a little more protected from the elements. The white folks moving into the neighborhood named it after themselves, Pioneer Square.

Later, as the neighborhood evolved into a town, the settlers decided to show their appreciation for all the hospitality and free stuff they got from Chief Si'ahl and named their little town Seattle.

Not long after the settlement was born, a man named Henry Yesler rolled in and established a sawmill on the nearby waterfront. With an abundance of quality Evergreen fir trees all around and even *in* the new town, Yesler had no problem getting the logs to his mill. He used horses, mules, and oxen to skid the logs down a hill to his tree slaughterhouse. The trail became known as, 'Skid Road'. At the time, the words, skid road, didn't carry any negative connotations but we learn later how the words evolved into a generic term for a scuzzy address.

As the mill prospered and more settlers rolled into the region, relations with the some of the Indians became strained. *No, really!*

Some disgruntled Indians started moving away from the white folks' town. Out to the country as it were. The ones that moved away mad became known as 'bad' Indians. The Indians that worked with the settlers and stayed in the encampment were 'good' Indians.

Chief Si'ahl tried in vain to smooth things out but relations deteriorated to the point of war. In 1856 the 'Battle of Seattle' took place. Not much of a battle really. Shots were fired by the 'bad' Indians toward the settler's stockade but the deplorable Indians didn't try to advance. Unfortunately, the settlers suffered two casualties when a fourteen-year-old boy and a panicked settler wandered into the line of fire.

Washington was a territory then, and as such, had its first Territorial Governor, Isaac Stevens. Stevens was also appointed Superintendent of Indian Affairs for the territory. With tensions running high between Indians and settlers, Stevens was under a lot of pressure from President Pierce to push treaties through as fast as possible. He was pretty much given a free hand on how that was accomplished.

Here, Mr. Indian. Just mark an X on this document and we'll give you all the whiskey you want. We'll even throw in some righteous religion too! Then maybe, *Oh, look, your moccasin's untied.*

Not sure if the Indians had a term for, dirty bastard, but the name Isaac Stevens may have worked, especially after Stevens declared martial law on the area and proposed a bounty on all 'bad' Indian scalps.

An historian summed up the state of affairs during Stevens' reign, "The killing of an Indian was no greater consequence than shooting a cougar or a bear." It didn't really matter that Indians may have lived in the area for ten thousand years, maybe even before cougars and bears. This attitude toward Indians continued and became so irrational that in 1865, when Seattle held its first-ever town council meeting, they voted to make it illegal for Indians to enter the city. *But hey, thanks for the waterfront property!*

It's hard to beat the $27 for Manhattan deal, but it seems like the Seattle thing was right up there too.

A lot of what Swannie learned pissed him off as a human being, it was disturbing for sure, but was it enough to put him off as a potential businessman? Should past social injustices be just that, past? Just because Christian missionaries decided to outlaw Native religion back then, it was no scalp off of his head now, right? Why did he care that the white monks told the Indians that totem poles were blasphemy and that they should be destroyed? It's the twentieth century now. Bidness is bidness, right? Swannie thought that maybe he would install a totem pole in his new place to show he was a good sport.

This rationale took Swannie through the good and bad times of Pioneer Square's history. In the beginning the square evolved into a bustling mecca for businesses.

Trading companies, supply houses, marine chandlery, and a few restaurants and hotels. But when businesses started moving *out* of Pioneer Square for an even better locale, the center of Seattle shifted to the north, leaving vacant buildings behind. However, these buildings didn't stay empty for long. Parlor houses, gambling joints, opium dens, flop houses, pawnshops, saloons, and tattoo parlors, soon occupied most of the area.

Crime became rampant. It became so dangerous in Pioneer Square at one point that the local gendarmes would only patrol the area in pairs or teams. Seattle did have a police force but was run by a corrupt police chief who often looked the other way when complaints were made and was known to take a bribe or two.

Nevertheless, at the time, there was one saloon that cops could go to and feel relatively safe, it was called 'Our House'. Our House was unique in that it doubled as a place where safety deposit boxes could be rented. It was rumored that Seattle's police chief made a deal with the denizens of Pioneer Square; "Don't screw with 'Our House', and I won't screw with yours."

Swannie fast forwarded his thinking and wondered if safety deposit boxes would work in a sports bar.

After a while, Swannie finally decided he'd researched enough. He called Masin and set up a time to meet.

CHAPTER THIRTY-ONE

Ben Masin was in his middle fifties and an easy man to talk to. He seemed pleased that a young man was interested in renting his place to start a new business. As he showed Swannie the space, he explained that it used to be a liquor store and was actually part of Masin's old furniture store. If Swannie wasn't sold on the place before, he certainly was when Masin showed him the storage area below ground level that came with the lease. It was vacant expect for an up-right piano that looked like it was still in decent shape.

Masin confirmed the condition of the piano by playing a few cords. He said he would donate the piano to Swannie if he leased the place.

Swannie could visualize the storage space seating another two hundred people. He saw a stage where he could bring in live entertainment. The ground floor could serve as his sports bar/restaurant.

When they were back upstairs, Masin started pointing out other amenities that might be beneficial to opening a sports bar. Swannie cut him off by saying; "I'll take it."

"Great," Masin said. "I'll draw up the lease agreement and as soon as you can make the deposit we'll be in business."

Swannie nodded his head, "No problem, I'll take it."

The two men walked back upstairs and out to the street. After Masin locked the front door they shook hands and agreed to meet in two days. As Masin walked away, Swannie stood on Second Street smiling and looking at the building that would house his first business venture. Now, all he had to do was find the money to make it happen.

Peters was the first to turn him down, saying his money was tied up at the moment but if he could wait a couple of months, maybe he could help. The second person to turn him down was a buddy from college who had just started up his own sports bar in Ellensburg, Washington.

Swannie stalled Masin, telling him he was really busy at work but would get by Masin's office to sign the lease and give him the deposit as soon as he could get free. On his third try Swannie got lucky and found someone that was able and willing to take a chance with him. On a handshake and his word, Swannie borrowed five thousand dollars from his former little league coach, Doug Berke. The Swandog was in business.

After quitting his job at Peter's Inn, Swannie got busy on his own place. He got bids from different contractors and lined up some worker bees. Choosing the right place for the kitchen was a challenge, but because some plumbing and electrical were already in place downstairs, that's where the kitchen went. Swannie also had a small office built downstairs in one corner and a VIP table in the opposite corner. An existing red brick wall that oozed dirty old mortar served as the perfect backdrop for the stage that was constructed. When it came time to install the carpet over the slab, the piano had to be moved. One of the workmen named Felix called Swannie who was home sick at the time, and asked where he should do with the piano. Since space was somewhat limited downstairs, Swannie decided to put the piano upstairs, near the back bar.

Swannie knew the man he was speaking to was possibly an illegal without papers but didn't care about that at the time.

"Take the piano upstairs and set it by the bar," Swannie said. "De bahrr?" Replied Felix.

"Yeah. Take it...ah, you know, how do you say, up? Areeba, or something like that, go up, above, okay? Comprende? Upstairs, by the bar!"

"Oh, si. Okay-dokey. Muy bien."

Two days later Swannie was feeling better and drove down to his project. As he walked through the front door, he stopped to admire what had been done so far. The new hardwood flooring was finished and looking good. Chairs, tables, mirrors, and a stand-up bar had been brought in. Swannie let his gaze drift back to the small alcove above the back bar where he planned on installing at least two televisions and maybe a... *Whoa!*

Holy shit!

Swannie had a hard time believing what he was seeing. Sitting neatly against the recessed wall and about seven feet off the floor sat the piano. Stunned, Swannie slowly sat down and tried to figure out how and why it got there. About that time Felix came by smiling. "Es everthin okey-dokey, hefe?"

"I...I dunno...how did you get the piano up there?" "I thogh you tol me to put above bahr. You no like?"

Swannie was still trying to digest the situation when he noticed an old block and tackle lying on the floor. And then for some reason he thought of the apostrophe on the Mavericks' bus. He smiled said, "No, it's okay. It looks good there. Leave it." Traditionally when construction crews finish framing a house or building, they place a tree on the ridge cap for good luck. Swannie figured he needed all the luck he could get with his project and wanted to do something like that as well. The first thing he thought about was a totem pole. The natural place for it would have been outside the front door but there had been a recent vandalism of a totem pole just two blocks away. If he put a totem pole inside the bar, it would take up valuable space. Then he had a thought; why do totems have to be in vertical order? Why not a horizontal totem...pole?

In the end, Swannie hired a local Indian to carve a horizontal totem. It was comprised of twelve swans all swimming in the same direction and installed lengthwise above the main entry door. When asked why he did it that way Swannie replied, "I like to keep all my swans in a row."

CHAPTER THIRTY-TWO

One of the first things an owner of a sports bar needs to do before he can open is find a sales representative for beer deliveries. Swannie didn't have to look very far, in fact he didn't have to look at all when a beer rep showed up at his door. The man was Sonny Sixkiller, former University of Washington starting quarterback among other things.

Sixkiller was born in Tahlequah, Oklahoma and was a member of the Cherokee Nation. His family had moved to Ashland, Oregon when he was just a year old. Sixkiller later attended Ashland High and was a natural athlete, lettering in all major sports. In football he played quarterback and was selected to the All-Southern Oregon Conference and to the Second Team All-State. In basketball he made All-Conference as a point guard and All-Conference in baseball as a pitcher. Oh, and he was also popular in school and was a good student. (Don't you just love those kinda guys?)

In college, Sixkiller garnered a lot of ink on sports pages and made the cover of several sports magazines, including *Sports Illustrated*. And, if it wasn't for his size, 5'11, 170 lbs., we would probably be including some memorable anecdotes from a professional career.

Swannie and Sixkiller hit it off immediately. Besides the similarities in physical size, age, and their history of athletics, they both had a sense of humor.

In an effort to schmooze Swannie as a client, Sixkiller got Swannie out on the golf course. They played the West Seattle Public Course, which is located in West Seattle of all places, and has a fantastic view of the city. They were playing with another twosome but giving it to each other as if there were nobody else around. "You play golf like old people fuck," Swannie told Sixkiller on about the third hole. Six was quick on the draw though, "Yeah? Well, you play golf like Custer's last cluster-fuck!"

So, it went until they reached the par-five thirteenth hole. The tee shot on that hole required a blind drive over a hill that was about hundred yards straight ahead. To the left was a rickety cyclone fence that paralleled the fairway, signifying out of bounds and semi-protecting a row of houses that reached all the way down the fairway to the green. Swannie was the last to tee off, and when he did, he sliced one up over the hill to the left. (Remember, to a lefty, hitting the ball to the left is a slice. See how screwed up southpaws can be?)

Right after Swannie hit his drive, one of the other players said, "Did you hear that?

Sounded like a yelp. Like maybe your ball hit an animal or something." Sixkiller; "Couldn't been a birdie. He's never hit one of those in his life."

The foursome walked up over the hill and found three balls in the fairway. Swannie's was nowhere to be seen. Sixkiller and Swannie walked along the high fence line until they spotted a dog lying in the backyard of one of the houses. They also saw Swannies' ball lying next to it. The dog looked like an older Bulldog mix. He had a lump on his forehead just above an eye. He didn't appear to be breathing.

"Oh my god." Swannie said. You don't think...?"

Sixkiller picked up a stick and tossed it at the dog. Nothing.

After calling to the dog and throwing more sticks and pinecones, an older man came out of the slider door of the house. He didn't look happy. "What the hell's goin' on here?" he said.

"Well sir, I don't know," answered Swannie. "I may have hit your dog with my golf ball."

The man grunted and shuffled over to the dog. He bent over the animal and looked at it. Then he poked it with his foot.

"You hit him all right. He's dead'ern hell."

Nobody said anything for a second and then Swannie; "Aw, Jesus man. I'm really, really, sorry."

The old man just looked at him with a scowl on his face.

"Here," Swannie said. "Let me give you my card. I own a restaurant downtown. I'll make it up to you somehow, I promise. God, I'm really sorry."

The old man grunted and said, "Don't be sorry, son. That was my wife's dog. Mean sum bitch. I been tryin' to get rid of it ever since my wife left three years ago."

"Wha...?"

"You go on," the old guy said. "I'll take care of it." Swannie looked at Sixkiller. "What should I do?"

Six shrugged, "I dunno. Take two strokes and hit one from here, I guess."

(photo: Sue Swanson)

Swannie at his bar with Sonny Sixkiller and beer reps

CHAPTER THIRTY-THREE

When Swannie had his grand opening on April 21, 1980, there were plenty of sports bars in and around Seattle. And why not? The fans understood that expansion teams probably weren't going to bust out of the gates and win anything right away, but they didn't care. They had big league teams to cheer for now. Their time would surely come.

Most of the sports bars had several televisions positioned throughout, pool tables, beers galore, burger baskets and appetizers. Waitresses in short skirts and jerseys in the colors of local teams. Sponsors of softball teams. Busy bartenders. All good stuff.

But without even trying, Swannies was soon developing something the other sports bars in the area didn't have; a clientele of professional athletes, past and present.

Sonny Sixkiller may have started the ball rolling by telling his friends and other former jocks about Swannies and then hanging out there himself. And it didn't hurt when Dave Heaverlo, relief pitcher for the Mariners in 1980, started dropping in after games.

Actually, Heaverlo had graduated from Central University in 1973, two years ahead of Swannie. Although the two really didn't know each other at Central they both met up at school reunion and got to know each other.

When Heaverlo started coming into Swannies, he'd already traveled around the country having pitched successfully for the San Francisco Giants and the Oakland Athletics. He probably did more for Swannie's ego and confidence than anybody else when he said, "You know, when you travel around different cities with a professional baseball team, you invariably find out where the best watering holes are. From my experience, I can honestly say that Swannies was one of the best, if not thee best, place to go after a game." High praise from a guy that pitched and partied in cities like New York, Chicago, and Los Angeles.

Heaverlo was a bit of character himself. In his rookie year he shaved his head and insisted he keep his non-roster number and pitched with number 60 on his back. Sounds a little like Bouton, no?

Anyway, like Bouton, Heaverlo was no slouch on the mound either. By the time his career was over he had made 356 major league appearances, all as a relief pitcher, and compiled an ERA of 3.41.

One of the things Heaverlo and other pros liked about coming into Swannies was that Swannie always went out of his way to protect players and celebrities that were in his place to relax and have a good time. There was a sign above the back bar that read, 'No pictures or autographs please.' Still, there were some autographs asked for and received, but for the most part, the people who came into Swannies were very respectful. For some of the players, it was a respite from signing everything people thrust in front of them; baseballs, hats, bats and boobs.

CHAPTER THIRTY-FOUR

On May 6th, 1981, the Seattle Mariners hired Rene Lachemann to replace Maury Wills as their third manager (Darrel Johnson was the Mariners' first manager in 1977.) Lachemann didn't have any major league managing experience, but the M's were willing to take that chance. As a team, they had yet to experience a winning season. Besides, Lachemann had served as bat boy for Tommy Lasorda and the Dodgers in 1962, so that had to count for something, right?

Actually, Lachemann came from a baseball family and by the time he had signed with Seattle as manager, he had been in a baseball uniform longer than most of the Mariners had been alive. In '64 he had signed a bonus contract with the Kansas City Athletics, and started working his way up through the minors, playing alongside Tony LaRussa and Dave Duncan. He eventually played one full season in the Majors as a catcher and pinch hitter with the A's. In his first appearance in the big leagues he was picked off second base and finished his playing career with a .210 batting average. Since he was too old to return to batboy status, he turned to managing in the minors. He was in Seattle's minor league system when he was called up to manage the M's.

Lachemann, or 'Lach' to many, had good baseball sense along with people skills.

Players liked him and played hard for him. And, as oxymoron-ish as this sounds, Lachemann was deemed somewhat successful in his first partial season because the team had the best winning percentage in their history-.447. *Winning percentage?*

One day, Lachemann and a few of his coaches came into Swannies after a game. As usual Swannie was making the rounds making sure people were having a good time. One of the coaches knew Swannie and introduced to Lachemann. Stop me if you've heard this before, but the two former athletes had things in common and hit it off.

They started talking baseball trivia and records that will probably never be broken. Of course, they brought up Joe DiMaggio's 56 game hitting streak in 1941 (he also got a hit that year in the All-Star game, but it didn't count toward the record). Joltin' Joe also hit in 61 straight games in 1933 while playing in the Pacific Coast League, but the minor league record is 69 held by Joe (who?) Wilhoit set in 1919.

While they were jabbering, Swannie brought up another record of sorts that hopefully will never be broken. It was set by Philles' Richie Asburn with two swings of the bat. While at the plate in a game, Asburn hit a foul ball into the stands that hit a woman in the face and broke her nose. As the woman was being attended to by medical personnel, Asburn stepped to the plate and fouled off another ball that hit her again! (baseballreference.com)

When the two started talking about great catchers of the past, Swannie suddenly squatted into a crouch position and came up firing an imaginary strike to second.

Lach: "Looks like you still got an arm."

Swan: "Oh, yeah. No shit. I still got it. Besides catching, I played a lot of outfield too.

College and pro."

Swannie pantomimed a throw from the outfield as if to confirm.

Lachemann looked at Swannie for a minute and then said, "Wait a minute. Let's see that catcher's snap again."

After Swannie went through his motion, Lachemann said, "Bullshit! You're not a catcher. You're throwing left-handed!"

Swannie rolled his eyes. "Boy, nothin' gets by you does it? That must be why they made you manager!? I *told* you I was a catcher for the Portland Mavericks."

Lachemann held up his hands in mock surrender. "That's right you did. I'm sorry. It just seems weird to see a catcher move like that. A lefty and all."

Swannie shrugged. "Ah, that's okay. I'm used to it."

Lachemann studied Swannie some more and then asked, "You ever pitch?"

Swannie said, "A little. You know, just foolin' around. Like sometimes when my pitcher couldn't throw a curveball? I'd throw one back to him. Show him what one looks like. You know, pis him off a little."

Lachemann laughed. "I remember the time Johnny Bench was getting a little annoyed with his pitcher for not throwing hard enough. To prove his point, Bench called for a fastball and then caught it with his bare hand."

The two shared a few more stories and then Lach laid one on Swannie. "Think you could pitch batting practice?" "You mean for the Mariners?" "Yeah. I could use a lefty." "No shit?"

"No shit. Come on down. Give it a try." "Would I get paid?" "Would you care?" "No."

"Well, there you go. We'll be in town until Sunday night. Think you could come down to the park tomorrow around three?"

"Sure."

"Okay. If you still have a glove, bring it." "Does this mean I've made it to the Majors?"

Lachemann laughed. "You haven't made anything yet. I'm just sayin' I'll give you a look."

CHAPTER THIRTY-FIVE

The next day, Swannie was as excited as a Little Leaguer trying out for the team as he approached the Kingdome with glove in hand. A security guard let him in the stadium and directed him to the field. There were a few players milling around and batting cage was set up. A right-handed pitcher was tossing BP.

Swannie spotted Lachemann talking to a player he remembered from his days in Single A. The player was Dave Henderson, the first draft pick in the history of the Mariners franchise. Lachemann waved Swannie over to them. "Hendu, this is Jim Swanson, owner of Swannie's. I've invited him over to---"

"I know this knucklehead," Henderson interrupted, "He played for the Portland Mavericks when I was first drafted and played in Bellingham."

Henderson's wide, tooth-gaped smile gave him away as an ally. "He gave me shit for being a bonus baby the first time I came to the plate, you remember that, Swandog?"

Swannie looked down and kicked the dirt. "Yeah, I remember all right. You came up to bat and swung at a couple of pitches and missed. Bouton was pitching and I yelled something to him like, "Hey Bulldog, looks like this bonus baby is more baby than bonus."

Henderson, still smiling, said, "That's right. Then what happened?" "And then you crushed one outta the park, asshole." "That's right," Henderson said, smiling even wider. "It was one of my first home runs in professional baseball. And then what happened, you know, when I was rounding the bases?"

Swannie looked away for a second, and then said slowly and begrudgingly, "Bouton tipped his hat to you. I'm still pissed he did that."

Lachemann laughed, and slapped Henderson on the back. "Alright, why don't you get in the cage and see if Swannie can get the ball across the plate." Then to Swannie; "Try not to hit him, okay?"

The first few pitches Swannie threw were standard 'fast' balls' that were right down the middle of the plate and topped out at about 68 mph. After Henderson parked a couple of them, he yelled to Lachemann "Sign him. This is fun!"

Swannie picked the next ball out of the bucket and yelled to Henderson. "Oh yeah? I haven't put any juice on anything yet. See if you can catch up to this one, hotshot."

Swannie took a full wind-up like he was going to try and power one by Henderson but threw a knuckleball instead. Henderson whiffed.

"How you like me now, Jack?" Swannie asked.

Henderson laughed and gave him the finger. Lachemann laughed and gave Swannie the job.

(photo: Sue Swanson)

Swannie and Hendu

Not everybody was happy with Lachemann's decision to bring in a new lefty for batting practice. A week or so after 'making the club' Swannie had just finished pitching BP and was walking by Lachemann's office door. Lach spotted him and yelled, "Hey, Swannie, come in here for a sec."

In the room with the skipper was a guy that the Mariners had acquired in a trade several months before hand. The guy was actually part of one of those, 'player to be named later,' deals, but we'll call him 'Bob' for now. Bob seemed to be agitated about something. Swannie's instincts told him there might be trouble ahead.

As Swannie walked in, Bob quickly walked out without making eye contact or saying anything. Swannie looked at Lachemann. "What's up Skip?"

Lach leaned back in his chair and folded his hands together. "Well, I just got a complaint about you, and I'm not sure how to handle it."

"A complaint? For what? What'd I do now?" "You know, 'Bob', that guy that was just in here?" "Yeah, well, I mean, I don't really know him..."

"He said you hit him with a pitch during batting practice today." Swannie looked stunned.

"Yeah. So?"

Lach leaned forward and scratched his head. "So, I've got to figure out how to keep everybody happy around here."

Swannie was dumbfounded. "It was a fucking curveball for Christ's sake's!"

Lachemann raised his hands in defense, saying, "I know, I know. But as manager of this club, I have to maintain a certain amount of discipline. Sometimes I have to make decisions I don't like. You know what I mean?"

Swannie looked at the ceiling and swore under his breath.

Lachemann continued, "So anyway, here's what I'm thinking; if it comes up that you have to pitch to Bob again, just throw everything outside and make him reach for it. If he complains, tell him you're trying to intentionally walk him."

It took Swannie a second or two to realize Lachemann was just screwing with him.

As it was, Swannie didn't have to pitch to Bob again. Mainly because 'Bob' was traded shortly thereafter.

Another person that took an interest in the Mariners' batting practice was Dave Niehaus. Niehaus was the Mariners play-by-play radio announcer who had begun his career with Armed Forces Radio before teaming up with Dick Enberg to broadcast California Angels games. The Mariners hired Niehaus in 1977 as their inaugural broadcaster and he always liked to get to the park early to watch some B.P. and to prep for his show. He was on the field when Swannie made his debut as batting practice pitcher and noticed the repartee between player, manager, and the new lefty.

When Niehaus asked Lachemann about his new 'pitcher', Lach called Swannie over and made the introductions. Neither man knew it at the time, but it would turn out to be the beginning of a nice relationship. Niehaus would soon be stopping by Swannies for an après game drink and Swannie would occasionally be spotted in the broadcast booth having a smoke with his new pal before games.

Their relationship developed to the extent that the following year, Niehaus began flying Swannie and his father down to Arizona to join him for spring training.

CHAPTER THIRTY-SIX

In just his second year, Swannie's had become *thee* place to be, especially after sporting events. Although NBA and NFL players were dropping by in-season, you were more likely to run into a pro baseball player hanging there, mostly because of their long-ass season. Sometimes they behaved themselves, sometimes they didn't.

One night in '81, the Chicago White Sox were in town, managed by Lachemann's old buddy, Tony La Russa. After the game, several of the Sox's strolled over to Swannies, including La Russa and his newly acquired designated hitter, Greg Luzinski.

Luzinski was a big boy who stood 6'1 and weighed 255. His nickname of 'The Bull' was accurate. 'Crusher' would have worked just as well. In his time in Chicago, Luzinski literally hit the roof of Cominsky Park three times. His home runs were prodigious blasts.

Before he joined the White Sox, Luzinski had been in the Majors for ten years, all with the Philadelphia Phillies where he played left field. Luzinski didn't particularly play the position well, but during one stretch he batted over three hundred in three consecutive years, was a three-time All Star and MVP runner-up in '75 when he led the league in RBI. With those kinds of numbers, he could be forgiven for his soft defense.

Besides, how many people named 'Bull' are light on their feet?

Now, playing in the American League as a designated hitter, he didn't have to worry about his fielding skills. In the four years that he would play for the Sox, he would be chosen as Designated Hitter of the Year, twice.

Another prize that Luzinski won was the Roberto Clemente Award which is given to the Major League player that best exemplifies the game of baseball, sportsmanship, commitment to his team, and community involvement. We mention this award because of the following anecdote may seem out of character for someone who was obliviously well liked by his peers.

The night in question started out well enough at Swannies, but it soon headed south.

The Sox had lost the game and Luzinski wasn't absorbing it well. What he was absorbing, was way too much alcohol. There were a few Mariners in the crowd and the trash talking was escalating to the point Swannie was growing concerned about his furniture.

Lachemann and La Russa were downstairs at the VIP table and listening to a local band, when Swannie went down and told La Russa that Luzinski was getting loud and hard to control upstairs. La Russa went up and had a talk with his player, assured Swannie things were cool and then went back downstairs. Twenty minutes later, Swannie sent for the Sox' skipper again. The 'Bull' needed to exit the corral before he broke it down.

By the time La Russa came back upstairs Luzinski was bellowing and giving everyone in the place shit. La Russa, who would later earn four Manager of the Year awards, got Luzinski to calm down somewhat and suggested that he take a taxi back to his hotel.

When the cab showed up, La Russa walked Luzinski by the arm out to the car. Just when it looked like everything was under control and the Roberto Clemente Award was kicking in, La Russa let go of Luzinski's arm for a moment to give the driver instructions. Luzinski went around to the passenger side and reached for the door handle to get in. Unfortunately, the driver, who was wearing a turban and looked to be from India, had yet to unlock the door. Luzinski pulled on the handle but nothing happened.

He pounded on the window glass and pulled again, but the driver was distracted listening intently to La Russa's instructions. This was like a red flag for the Bull. Enraged, he snorted, cussed, and ripped the door handle completely off of the car. This got the drivers attention. He punched the gas pedal and shot out of there like he was in a 'Roadrunner' cartoon. *"Meep, Meep!"*

A couple of Seattle's finest in a cruiser just happened to pull up just as this was going down. They were no strangers to Swannies, not because it was a trouble spot, but because they were regulars there themselves. In fact, they were on a first name basis with Swannie, who stepped outside the front door just in time to run interference.

"Trouble here, Swannie?" asked one of the cops as he stepped out of his cruiser. "Nah, just a little miss-understanding, officer."

The cop looked at Luzinski who was standing there with the door handle still in his hand. Fortunately, 'The Bull' wasn't saying a word.

"Yeah, I can see that," the cop said." He turned to Swannie. "You want to tell us what happened?"

Swannie scratched his head. "Umm, yeah, well, you see sir, Mister Luzinski here, whom I'm sure you know plays for the Chicago White Sox, and, well, ah, you know, he was just trying to get a ride to his hotel. They've got a day game tomorrow. and he wanted to be well rested. Probably gonna be signing a lot of autographs for the kids tomorrow too, you know."

The cop knew he was being hustled but asked, "So, why'd he rip the door handle off?"

"Well, sir, you see, ah, Greg here just wanted to sit in the front. But the door was locked."

"So, he ripped the handle off?"

"Well, yes sir. But he didn't mean to...it's just that..."

LaRussa stepped in and said, "It's just that Mr. Luzinski gets carsick if he has to ride in the back."

Swannie looked at LaRussa like he was the genius that he was and is, and then said, "That's right, officer. Just a little miss-understanding."

When the two cops looked at each other and shrugged, Swannie knew the situation was under control. So, Swannie being Swannie, pressed his luck and asked his buddies, "Any chance you guys could give Mister Luzinski a lift? I know my friend, Tony, here, would appreciate it. Right, Tony?"

"You bet. And if you guys are baseball fans, or your kids are, I can get you tickets for tomorrow's game?"

Five minutes later the patrol car left with Mister Luzinski smiling and riding in the front seat.

CHAPTER THIRTY-SEVEN

Not all the baseball players that came into Swannies were as strong or intimating as Luzinski, but one fellow does come to mind, especially when you include determination; and that man is Kirk Gibson. When Gibson came into Swannies, you'd thought Wyatt Earp had just sauntered in. Not that Gibson thought of himself that way, but there was a certain raw energy about him that made people look his way, at least once.

Gibson went to Michigan State University, where he was an All-American wide receiver in football and garnered All-American honors. While at State, one of the football coaches advised him to try-out for baseball to help stay limber during football's off-season. So, Gibson played one year of baseball for the Spartans, stayed loose, hit .390 with 16 homers and 52 RBI in 48 games.

After graduation, Gibson was drafted number seven by the St Louis Cardinals football team (now the Arizona Cardinals) and number one by the Detroit Tigers baseball club. Throw in being elected to the Collage Football Hall of Fame, and you get an idea of what kind of athlete we're talking about here. A left-handed one at that.

One night, Gibson came in by himself after a game. But instead of heading to the back of the room where the main bar was, he angled over to his left and studied the wall where twenty or thirty baseball bats were mounted. All the bats had name tags hanging below them. Gibson finally made his way to the bar where Swannie was working.

"Hey, Swannie." "Hey, Gibby."

Gibson, never one for small talk, asked, "How come you don't have one of my bats on your wall?" "Well, let's see," Swannie said. "Maybe it's because I never got a bat from you?" Gibson seemed to think it over for a moment. "You goin' to tomorrow's game?" Swannie: "I was thinkin' about it."

"Good. I'll get you a bat tomorrow."

The next day was Sunday and first pitch was scheduled for 1:10. Swannie hadn't really planned on going to the game but since Gibson had more or less invited him, he decided to go. Besides, there was a girl that Swannie was interested in, so he asked her to go with him. Swannie had season tickets that he usually handed out to customers. They were great seats, only a few rows back from the field near the visitors' on-deck-circle. If nothing else, the view should impress the young lass.

Swannie and his date where just settling into their seats when the game started.

Detroit was up first of course, and Gibson was scheduled to bat third. The first batter popped out, which brought Gibson to the on-deck-circle. He had two bats in his hands.

Swannie nudged his date and pointed at Gibson. "See that guy? That's Kirk Gibson.

He's going to give me one of his bats so I can hang it on my wall over at my place." "Really?"

Not wanting the lady to doubt him, Swannie yelled over to Gibson, "Hey, Gibby, one of those bats is for me, right?"

Gibson was busy watching the pitcher's motion while subconsciously wind-milling both bats around his torso and stretching. When the Detroit batter lined-out to the first baseman, Gibson tossed one of the bats down and walked to the plate. Just as he dug in to the batter's box, Swannie yelled again only louder this time. "Don't forget my bat, pal!"

Gibson suddenly called time, put one foot out of the box, waggled his bat a couple of times, and then flipped it upside down and then tapped the handle on home plate, checking for a crack. Apparently, something was off because Gibson turned and started back toward the dugout with his bat in his left hand. Just as he neared the on-deck circle Swannie yelled to him again.

"Hey Gibby. I don't want no cracked bat, you know?"

Gibson stopped, spotted Swannie, and said, "Well, here, check it out."

And with a flick of his wrist, Gibson sent the bat flying into the stands right to Swannie.

The next day at Swannies, Gibson's bat was proudly on display, crack and all.

CHAPTER THIRTY-EIGHT

The Seahawks were in their fourth year of existence, and already had winning records in two of those years. Not bad for an expansion team. In fact, the Seahawks had made their Monday Night Football debut the year before, playing against the Atlanta Falcons thrilling a national audience by coming from fourteen points down, scoring on a fake field goal, and eventually winning the game 31-28. All this prompted Howard Cosell to exclaim, "The Seahawks are giving the Nation a lesson in entertaining football!"

While the Seahawks were gaining popularity, Swannie's reputation was growing as well. Not only was Swannies a good place to hang out after games, it was a good spot to grab a Bloody Mary and something to eat before games.

One Sunday before a Seahawks game, a party of eight young men came in and sat down for lunch. About half of them wore Seahawks' paraphernalia and they were obviously going to the game that day. Just before the 1:00 kick-off, the boys finished their meal and walked out, heading for the Kingdome. When Swannie went over to help the waitress clean up their table, she seemed upset. "The cheap bastards didn't even leave a tip," she said.

Swannie grabbed the lunch receipt from the waitress and hustled out after the guys. He caught up to them has they were crossing the street and asked the man he guessed had signed for lunch, "Excuse me sir? Was everything all right with your meal?"

A slight man about thirty years old, somewhat nerdy looking with light brown hair, glasses and a wry smile, looked at Swannie. "Yes. It was fine. Why?"

"Because," Swannie said, "I have a sweet waitress back there that thinks she may have done something wrong." Swannie showed him the receipt and said, "The meal was a hundred and forty-five bucks, but there was no tip. What's up with that?"

The man looked at the receipt and frowned. One of his friends yelled at him; "C'mon, Bill, we're gonna be late."

Still standing in the middle of the street, 'Bill' took out a pen, wrote something on the receipt, and handed it to Swannie. "I'm sorry, I thought my friends were leaving the tip."

Huh-huh, Swannie thought, he'd heard that one before. As he watched the man walk away, he looked at the slip in his hand. The tip was for two hundred dollars. Swannie called after him, "Atta boy, Bill! You all come back now, you hear?"

When Swannie got back to his place and told the waitress what happened she couldn't believe it. "Do you know the guy or something?"

Swannie smiled and said, "Bill? Yeah, me and him are buds now." He handed her the receipt and walked away. The waitress looked at the name on it, studied it for a moment, and then asked herself, "Gates? Who's William H. Gates?"

CHAPTER THIRTY-NINE

The name Mike Hilderbrand might not mean anything to most people, but it does to Jim Swanson. Swannie met Hilderbrand while they were going to college at CWU. They became good friends and still are today. We bring Hilderbrand into this story because he was there from the start of 'Swannies', even helping with the remodel of the old liquor store. At times Hilderbrand served as unofficial bar manager and probably spent as much time at Swannies as anybody, including Swannie.

Hilderbrand witnessed many of the events that are included in this biography, some that Swannie wasn't even aware of until later. Hilderbrand became such a regular at the bar, Swannie assumed he was on the payroll. Swannie was never very good at some things, like knowing who was really working for him and who was a guest bartender. He signed all the paychecks because he had to. He never really looked at the names on the checks.

One night a fellow CWU alumnus named Pat Strong came into the bar looking for Swannie. Strong had been pals with Hilderbrand and Swannie while in college and was traveling around the state as a representative for Asics, maker of athletic shoes. Swannie wasn't working that night but Hilderbrand was there and joined Strong at the bar and began catching up on old times. About that time a man pulled up a stool next to them and ordered a drink. When the bartender came back with his drink, the man nodded toward the front window and said, "I just saw a guy hit the sign on the first try."

The bartender looked surprised. "Really? Wow. That's impressive. I don't think anybody's ever done that, not even Ron Guidry."

"Yeah, well he did it. I saw it. You owe him a drink. He threw a strike."

As the bartender turned away, he said over his shoulder, "That's good to hear, Don. It's about time you expanded your strike zone."

"Fuck you," the man named Don said.

Strong looked at Hilderbrand for an explanation. Hilderbrand laughed and quickly introduced Strong to the man sitting next to them.

"Don, this is a friend of mine, Pat Strong. Pat, this is Don Deckenger. Don is a Major League umpire for the American League. Works a lot of the Mariners games."

Strong was duly impressed. Like many of us, he had never met a professional umpire before and said so. Don laughed, "You stick around this place, you'll meet or see just about anything or anybody. It's like the 'Who's Who, of Major League Baseball.'"

Hilderbrand leaned in and added, "Don is also our unofficial 86-er here. If a customer gets a little too rowdy, Don just signals the bartender or doorman." Hilderbrand demonstrated an umpire's call for 'out'.

"So, what's this about some guy throwing a strike?" Strong asked. Hilderbrand smiled and explained. "I think it started with a couple of guys who had just walked out of the bar. They were standing on the sidewalk bullshitin', when someone from the kitchen walked by with a bunch of old lemons and limes they were gonna throw away. One of the guys grabbed a lemon and threw it at a pigeon that was sitting on a telephone pole nearby. He missed badly, and the bird flew away nonchalantly flew away. When his buddy spotted a seagull on the roof of a three-story building across the street, that became their new target."

Swannie saw what the guys were doing and walked outside and offered to buy either one of them a drink if they could hit the sign on top of that roof."

"What if a cop sees you?" Strong asked.

"A cop?The cops around here don't care." Hilderbrand said. "They usually toss a few themselves."

Strong laughed, shook his head, and wondered what kind of place he had come into.

As the night rolled on, Strong continued to throw back tequila shots, pausing just long enough to go outside and throw a few lemons at the building across the street.

After a couple of hours, Strong was toasted and in no shape to drive anywhere.

Finally, Hilderbrand convinced Strong to leave his car where it was and come home with him. "My girlfriend won't mind. The times I've brought an occasional stray dog home she says I'm helping them from getting hurt. You can sleep on the couch, just don't start howling. I'll bring you back in the morning."

The next day, after a Bloody Mary morning, Hilderbrand brought Strong back to the scene of the crime. Strong described the car that he was driving and the area he thought he had left it. After a couple of passes around the block, Strong spotted his car. The rear window had been smashed out.

"You leave anything in the car?" Hilderbrand asked. "My shoe samples. Twenty boxes, I think." Strong said.

After Hilderbrand parked his car, they walked up to Strong's car. There was broken glass in the back seat but nothing else. After a brief conversation, Strong decided he should call his employer and insurance company while Hilderbrand called the police. There was a set of phone booths nearby and the calls were made.

When the police arrived, they asked Strong to describe what was missing and what the stolen property was worth. They were astonished when Strong laughed and said, "Probably zero. The boxes only contained one shoe each. The left one. All of them white and in different sizes. That's how Asics wanted it. Protection against theft, I guess."

After mulling the situation over for a minute or two, Hilderbrand said he might have an idea where the stolen goods were. There was a homeless camp set up a couple of blocks up the hill on a small grassy area. If the cops were up for a short walk, he could take them there. The cops agreed and the four of them walked up the street.

When they reached the camp, they saw about a dozen homeless men sitting outside a tent. They all looked very stylish with one sparkling white athletic shoe on their left foot.

CHAPTER FORTY

Many times, people seemed to change when they walked into Swannies, not physically but metaphysically. It was like you could stomp your feet at the door, shake the dust and miseries off, and then come inside happy. People with 9-5 mundane jobs would loosen up and start conversations with other folks at the bar. Guards were let down and new friendships were started daily. Grumpiness stayed outside. Smiles and laughter were contagious. It was a level playing field and nobody was any better than anyone else. And that included Seattle's Finest.

Some of the beat cops took their breaks at Swannies. They would stroll in, grab a table and have a cup of coffee. If it was an afternoon break, sometimes they were served their java in a paper cup, no cream or sugar, but with an additive just the same.

A few off-duty police began frequenting Swannies in the evening as well. Many times, they stayed until the bell and beyond. The cops didn't have to disguise their drinks, but they kept their firearms covered. Most of the time anyway.

Swannie was normally the one who locked the doors and hosted the after-hours diversions. Occasionally, celebs, friends and maybe a good-looking gal or two could stay to help 'clean' the place. Sometimes an off-duty cop or two were part of the cleaning crew. Their presence never dampened the mood, quite the contrary. Folks knew the cops weren't there to bust anyone, they were just regular Joes like everyone else having a good time. If you wanted to do a line or two, or smoke something not recommended by the Surgeon General, just do it where the boys in blue didn't have to see you.

Once on a relatively quiet Thursday night, Swannie threw the keys to Hilderbrand and asked his friend to lock up for him. Hilderbrand was with his girlfriend, whom we'll call Rusty. Rusty was a good-looking woman, about 5' 7", long red hair and great legs. If you didn't count the gray matter in her head, she was the total package as some might say.

141

Most times when Swannie wasn't part of the after-hour crowd, there wasn't much of an after-hour crowd. Hilderbrand understood this and was cool with it. When he locked the doors that night there were a few people that were allowed to stay including a couple of cops, 'Dick' and 'Dan'.

An hour or so after official closing time, everybody had left except for Hilderbrand, Rusty, and the two cops. Even though it was just the four of them, they continued drinking downstairs at one of the tables near the stage. With every drink, Rusty seemed to become more enamored with boys in uniform. She would smile, bat her eye lashes and ask, "You ever shoot anybody? Are you married? Can I see your gun?"

After a while Hilderbrand knew he should steer his guests to the door but every time he brought it up Rusty would say something like; "Aw, come on, honey, one more for the ditch, please?" The two cops would shrug and look at Hilderbrand as if to say, "Hard to argue with a pretty redhead, right?"

Finally, Hilderbrand said, "Okay, one more, but that's it. I'm going upstairs to finish putting a few things away but when I'm done, we're outta here."

Hilderbrand went upstairs and began his final chores. He was just setting a bottle of premium scotch on the top self of the bar when he heard the gun shot from below.

He raced down downstairs and saw the three of them still at the table and laughing like hell. Rusty had her arm around cop 'Dick's shoulders, while cop 'Dan' had his service revolver out and pointing toward the stage where six bar stools had been set up. Five of the stools had bottles perched on top of them, one held nothing but shattered glass. The smell of cordite hung in the air.

"What the hell you doing!" Hilderbrand yelled.

"Just a little target practice," cop 'Dan' said. He was smiling from ear to ear.

Rusty leaned into one of those ears and said, "Show him."

Before Hilderbrand could say anything, Dan began firing again. The sound was deafening and Hilderbrand threw his hands over his ears. When the firing stopped, two bottles remained unscathed.

It was relatively quiet for a moment, and then Dick said, "You suck," He drew his pistol. 'Blam, blam, blam, blam.' Then there were none.

"Jesus H. Christ! The fuck you guys doin'?" Mr. Hilderbrand politely asked.

Rusty was slumped face down on the table with her arms stretched out in front of her.

Her upper body was jumping and convulsing. She was laughing hysterically.

"Jesus, Mike," cop Dick said. "Don't get so excited. Swannie didn't mind when we squeezed off a couple of rounds down here before!"

Hilderbrand was dumbfounded. "You're shittin' me? You guys do this all the time?"

Cop Dan laughed and said, "Well, no, not *all* the time. But we've plunked a few things down here when Swannie was with us."

Dick and Dan looked at each other as if to confirm it was no big deal, and then looked back at Hilderbrand. *What?*

Hilderbrand just shook his head. Then he thought about where he was and about his friend who owned the place.

Finally, Rusty raised her head, wiped her eyes, and tried to stop laughing. Cop Dick said, "Don't worry, we always clean up our mess. In fact, we have to account for every bullet we're issued, so we'll dig the slugs out before we leave, okay?"

Cop Dan had already gotten up and was walking toward the wall with a pocketknife in his hand. Hilderbrand sighed, shook his head again and went to find a broom. The next day when Hilderbrand walked into the bar, Swannie jumped all over him. "What the hell did you do after hours last night? Were the cops here?"

Hilderbrand stammered. ...."ah, well, not *cop* cops, but yeah, Dan and Dick stayed after..."

"Did they pull out their guns?"

"Yeah, well, I was upstairs setting up, and. "

"God damn it. What the hell's wrong with them?"

" ...uh, they told me they shot at shit here before and you didn't care then?"

"Oh, I don't care if they shoot at stuff, as long as they're pointing toward the fucking *brick* wall. Not at the wall *next* to it! That's just thin plywood. I've told them about that. The dumb bastards fired through the wall where we keep our liquor inventory. They killed some of my best whiskey!"

(photo: Rod Long)

Swannie not going quietly

(photo: Rod Long)

Swannie and Hildebrand in a mystery 'hand-witch'

CHAPTER FORTY-ONE

One day in 1982, a man walked into Swannies and asked to talk to the owner. Swannie could sense the man was going to try and sell him something, and he was right. The man's name was John Fox, he was from Los Angeles and he was selling talent. Comedy acts to be exact. The two sat at the bar and got right to business.

"Have you ever heard of, 'The Comedy Store'?" Fox asked.

"Is that where you buy condoms?" Swannie answered.

Fox laughed. "No, but I'd like to use that one if you don't mind."

"Use it for what, and where?"

"In a comedy act. On stage. Your stage." "You're a comedian?"

"No, but I can line you up with some good ones."

"Naw, I don't do comedy here. Just local bands downstairs. Got a dance floor. I do okay with it."

"Wanna do even better?" Fox asked

Typical salesman. Swannie thought. *I should just run him off.* But it was early afternoon and business was slow at that time, so he let the guy roll.

"It used to be if you wanted to see a good comedy you had to go to New York or Las Vegas, but since Johnny Carson moved his show outta New York to LA, there's lots of great acts showing up on the West Coast. You've heard of Cheech and Chong, haven't you?" Fox asked. "Maybe Jerry Seinfeld? I can bring them here. They're killin' it just about everywhere they go right now. Comedy acts are all the rage right now. If you work with me on this, you could have the first comedy club in the Northwest!" If Fox was anything, he was persistent.

Before Fox had walked in that day, Swannie was feeling pretty good about himself, thinking of the old adage; 'The first year in business is always the roughest. Survive that one and you've got a chance.' Now, in his second year, Swannie had every reason to be optimistic. With just word-of-mouth advertising, he had not only survived his first year, but was turning a profit, albeit a small one. He also knew he couldn't just rest on a 'rookie of the year' business status, he had to stay ahead of the curve. *Cheech and Chong? Jerry Sein-something.? Hmm..*

When Fox threw in a couple of other names of up-coming comedians he mentioned Bill Maher and Ellen DeGeneres.

Swannie, being the single hound-dog that he was, suddenly showed a little more interest in what Fox was saying. "Ellen DeGeneres? Is she that blonde? I think I've seen her on TV. She' cute."

"Yes, she is. *Showtime* just named her the funniest person in America."

"Really? How old is she?"

"Well, listen Mr. Swanson, why don't I fly you down to L.A. and show you around? We could take in a few shows and you can see for yourself what the fuss is all about, and who knows, maybe Ellen's hanging out at one of the clubs. You can ask her how old she is."

CHAPTER FORTY-TWO

A week later, Swannie was in L.A. with Fox, taking in the
sights, sounds, and laughter. Their first stop on the comedy scene
was Mitzi Shore's Comedy Store. They arrived early but there
was already a doorman on duty. He recognized Fox and waved
them in, thus avoiding a seven-dollar cover charge. Once inside
they looked around for a suitable table. The house lights were on
and Swannie could see that the place was only about a quarter
full and very quiet. He took note of the stage layout and other
seating arrangements. He also noticed the *Two drink minimum,*
placards on every table.

Once they were seated, Fox filled Swannie in. "After Carson
moved out here, stand-up comics started sprouting up all over
town, But Mitzi's was the place to be seen back then. Before she
bought it and remolded it to become 'The Comedy Store', it was a
popular nightspot called "Ciro's", where some of the biggest
celebs in Hollywood used to hang out. Brilliant marketing
strategy if you ask me. You know, setting up in a place like this
that was already popular with history. She even let some of the
struggling new comics that didn't have a pot to piss in stay here
and sleep on the couch."

"Really?" Swannie asked, picturing struggling deadbeats
spending the night downstairs in his place.

"Yeah," Fox said. "Mitzi was like the mother hen, nurturing
her flock. "A couple of the guys that earned couch time at Mitzi's
were David Letterman and Jay Leno. You heard of them?
They're rollin' pretty good right now."

"So, whaddya have to pay a comic?" Swannie asked. "How
much did what's-her-name pay them?"

"Funny you should ask. At first, Mitzi didn't pay them a
nickel to perform. The non-headliners anyway. It was sort of a
given that if you got to play 'The Comedy Store', that was
payment enough. It was where you honed your act, kinda like a
comedy camp. The comics did it because but there were always

scouts and agents in the audience looking for new talent. It was a place where you could launch your career."

"You mean I won't have to pay the comics anything?"

Fox laughed. "No, those days are gone. You have to pay just about everyone now. A few years ago, a bunch of the comics got together and threatened to strike if they weren't paid at least something."

By the time the first act started, The Comedy Store had filled up. Swannie looked around and started calculating what a two-drink minimum was bringing in. As the night went on, the audience became more and more lively and involved with the show.

Everyone seemed to be having a good time.

After watching two acts at The Comedy Store, Fox hustled Swannie over to the 'Improv' in Hollywood. It was more of the same. Lots of smiles and a big crowd peppered with celebs. Fox asked Swannie if he wanted to see some other night spots, but the answer was no. He'd seen enough. Swannie was sold on the idea of a comedy-club.

To this day Swannie cannot remember the names of the comics that played that night, he was too busy watching the crowd and their reactions, but he can say with certainty that in each place the two drink minimum signs were irrelevant.

Before flying back to Seattle the next day, Swannie reached a tentative verbal agreement with Fox; Fox would provide and manage all talent which included paying them. For this, Fox would receive all the revenue generated from a cover charge, aka, 'the door', plus ten percent of the booze. At first Swannie balked at the booze part of the deal, but later did the math and concluded that ninety percent of a full house was more than hundred percent of an empty one.

CHAPTER FORTY-THREE

Two months later, Swannie had completed the minor renovations he needed for the new and improved Swannies. He moved the kitchen around a little and set up a ticket booth at the bottom of the stairs to manage the cover charge. He did a minimum of advertising to announce his new enterprise, mostly just word of mouth and a poster in the window.

Three months after John Fox walked into Swannies, Swannie's opened as the first ever comedy-club in the Northwest. The first comic to stand up underground at the new club was Jerry Seinfeld.

On opening night Swannie was again more interested in the crowd than the talent on stage. He didn't really know much about Seinfeld but was putting his trust in John Fox. Swannie didn't expect to sell out the first night and wasn't disappointed when he didn't. After all, he hadn't done much to promote Seinfeld and considered opening night as more of a 'soft' opening than anything. But, still, there was a decent crowd that night and they seemed to appreciate the young comic on stage.

Seinfeld led off his act by saying how beautiful but remote the Pacific Northwest seemed to him. "It probably has something to do with me being born in Brooklyn, New York, I suppose." When nobody clapped or acknowledged his birthplace, he explained it was on the other side of America, four time zones away, and where the Dodgers used to play their home games.

He mentioned his father was of Hungarian Jewish descent and a big influence on him when he was a little boy. He father would often tell him jokes that he had remembered while serving in World War 11.

"So, I pretty much blame my parents for people laughing at me," Seinfeld said. "I also blame my parents for letting become left-handed. I'm always being put down for it. Left words are always negative things, like, *left*overs, two-*left*- feet, *left*-handed compliments? Ever heard of a crook named *Righty*? Everything *right* is a positive. The Bill of *Rights*! Right? *Right* on!

"You go to a party, there's nobody there. Where'd they all go? They *left*! You'd thought my parents woulda said something early on. Maybe like when I was in my highchair. 'Hey, Ma, he's tossing that mush with his left hand, make him throw righty for god's sake!' "

By now the crowd had warmed up considerably. When he asked if there were any left-handed people in the audience a few yipped and applauded. Seinfeld let the applause die down a little and then said. "Most of you may not know this, *but* in the very early times, all people on Earth were left-handed. Yep, it's true. It was back when everyone got along with each other and there was peace in the valleys. But then mankind invented weapons and everything changed. Everyone started carrying a club over their shoulder and not trusting one another other.

"But, ironically that's how the custom of people shaking hands began. For example, if two cavemen bumped into each other on the trail and weren't in the mood to fight, or maybe one was just in a hurry to get home, they would offer their right hand to show the other that he wasn't hiding anything in it, you know, like a rock or something. Of course, both guys still had a club over their left shoulder, so true peace remained nebulous at best."

Seinfeld let the polite laughter die down and then explained how today's society could benefit from history.

"So, I'm thinking, for the sake of world peace and friendship we should all start shaking hands *left*-handed from now on. You know, solidarity and all. And since Jim Swanson, the owner of this fine establishment, is already a southpaw, he may want to help promote the idea. All in favor, raise your left hand."

Needless to say, Seinfeld's idea never caught on and the movement for everyone to start shaking hands left-handed never made it outside of Swannie's.

However, that obliviously didn't diminish Seinfeld's rising star status. Shortly after appearing at Swannie's, he made his debut on The Johnny Carson Show and the rest they say is...well, you know.

CHAPTER FORTY-FOUR

There were a few times when Swannie would have to admonish some athletes or celebrities that took the, 'No pictures, No autographs' rules, too far. Players with large egos you might say.

One case involved Ricky Henderson, base-stealing whiz for the Oakland A's at the time and whose full name is Ricky Nelson Henley Henderson. (He was named after singer/actor Ricky Nelson. Go figure.)

Besides his base-stealing abilities, Henderson was known for his brash, fast talking, showboat style on and off the field. "I was born fast", he would say to anyone listening. The fact that he was born on Christmas Day in the backseat of an Oldsmobile on the way to the hospital endorses that theory.

Ricky Nelson Henderson was not a big man, more Swannie's size, but he was also a tremendous lead-off hitter with a good batting average and on base percentage. Part of his success at the plate could have been due to his unusual batting stance. He would crouch so low that it was hard to tell where his strike zone was. Or as the late-great sportswriter Jim Murray once said, "Ricky's strike zone is smaller than Hitler's heart."

The night in question, Henderson had been drinking and holding court at a table in Swannies when a small gray-haired lady approached his table. Henderson noticed her but didn't acknowledge her. He kept playing for his immediate audience...right up until the lady raised her Instamatic to take a picture of him. Then Henderson snapped. Quick as wink, he jumped up and shoved the camera into the lady's face (reminiscent of James Cagney pushing a grapefruit into Mae Clarke's face in the 1931 movie, *Public Enemy # 1*). Henderson barked at the woman, "No photos in here! Can't you read?"

The poor lady was startled of course and promptly backed away with her hands over her mouth. Swannie happened to be nearby and witnessed the whole thing. In a flash, he was all over Henderson. "What the hell you doin?"

"She was trying to take my picture, man! It's against the rules, right? Your sign says..."

Swannie, never one to mince words, especially when pissed, got face to face with Henderson and said from the heart, "I don't give a shit what the sign says! You just pushed an old lady for Christ's sake! You can't treat any of my customers like that!" Then like an umpire, Swannie thumbed Henderson out.

Ricky Henderson, a man not used to being thrown out, took it surprisingly well and left immediately. His departure may have been influenced by the fact that Dave, 'I'm-no relation-to Ricky', Henderson, aka Hendu, was standing directly behind Swannie when all of this took place. In the short time that Hendu and Swannie had known each other they had become good friends. Hendu was watching what was going down but without his trademark smile.

After the dust settled, Swannie went behind the bar, poured himself a drink and thought about what he'd just done. Had he really just tossed out a Major League star that held the record for stolen bases, was a batting near .300, and a leading candidate for the American League MVP that year? A guy that could probably pull out his wallet and buy and sell Swannie a hundred times over?

Hendu, who was now sitting at the bar across from Swannie, sensed his friend's anguish. "Don't worry about it, pal. He was out of line. You did the right thing. That's why we love you, man. Your balls are bigger than your brains! Besides, Ricky's not a bad guy, he just gets a little excited sometimes. He'll probably be back here tomorrow to apologize. I mean, who wants to be eighty-sixed from Swannies?"

Hendu, with his infectious smile, was hard to argue with.

And, sure as shit, to his credit, Ricky Henderson showed up the next day and apologized to Swannie.

Another player that Swannie had to explain the rules to one night was Seattle Supersonics' point-guard, Gary Payton. Before Payton began his NBA career with the Supersonics, he attended Oregon State University in Corvallis Oregon. In his senior year he was featured on the cover of *Sports Illustrated Magazine* as the nation's best college basketball player. After four years at OSU, Payton became one of the most decorated basketball players in the school's history. Take that Frank Peters!

Although Payton struggled early in his career with the Sonics, he soon developed into one of best point guards in the business and earned the nickname, "The Glove" for his defensive prowess. He also became known as one of the best trash talkers in the business and shared similarities with Ricky Henderson in the ego department.

Although the rule infraction that Payton committed wasn't as egregious as Ricky Henderson's, Swannie again had to step in and show who was boss. It happened while Swannie was upstairs behind the bar and Payton was downstairs at the VIP table supposedly enjoying the comedy act that was playing that night. The problem was Payton was being obnoxious with loud, nonstop chatter about himself and signing autographs for everyone around him. The manager downstairs asked Payton several times to keep it down so people could enjoy the show, but Payton just kept yakking' away, bobbing his head and jivin' like he was on the basketball floor.

Finally, Swannie was called in to mediate. He went downstairs and walked directly over to Payton. He didn't know what he was going to say to him, but he knew the man had to go.

"Having a good time, Gary?"

"Hell yes, man. Buy you a drink?"

"No, that's alright," Swannie said as he patted Payton on the back. "I just came down to...talk to you."

Then it hit him. "You're, ah, breaking one of the rules here you know."

"Wha, wha rule?"

"The autograph rule. See that sign over there? Just like the one upstairs. No autographs."

Payton looked confused for a moment, looked around at the crowd, then broke into a big smile.

"Aw, that's alright, man. They're cool. I don't mind. Nobody's bothering me."

Swannie shrugged and said, "Yeah, I know, man, but if I don't enforce the rule, I look like a dick, you know?"

Payton looked up at Swannie and his face fuzzed up again. Neither man said anything for a moment.

Then Payton put 8 and 6 together. "You're not throwin' me out, are you?"

Swannie laughed, "No Gary, I don't wanna throw you out...but I'm thinking about throwing you up."

"What? You're throwing me...where? Up?"

"Yeah. Up. Like in *up*stairs. Why don't you follow me topside? You can talk to the bartender up there all you want. He's a basketball fan. You can even slip him your autograph when nobody's looking."

Payton thought it over, smiled and decided that being thrown up was indeed better than being thrown out.

CHAPTER FORTY-FIVE

In 1983, the Chuck Knox era began for the Seattle Seahawks with the team advancing to their first ever play-off game. The football bar had now been set higher and expectations were rightfully flourishing. By 1986, the team had sniffed their first AFC Division Championship and Seattle fans found the fragrance intoxicating. They knew they had a good team in place and wanted more. If the club could just draft right and add a piece or two to their defense, they might just make it to the Promised Land.

At the time, Brian Bosworth, a two-time consensus All American linebacker from the University of Oklahoma, was eligible through the NFL's supplemental draft. Before the draft took place, Bosworth sent letters to teams that he didn't want to play for, which included Seattle.

In an interview with Bryant Gumbel on *The Today Show,* Bosworth said he would prefer to play for the Los Angeles Raiders because they fit his personality best. Hollywood being in the neighborhood may have had something to do with his thinking.

Seattle drafted him anyway. But then so did the Tacoma Stars of the Major Indoor Soccer League, saying, "Hey, Bosworth didn't send us a letter so we thought we'd give it a shot."

When Seattle came up with an offer of eleven million dollars, Bosworth changed his mind about playing for the Seahawks. The offer was the highest in team history and would also set a record for the highest rookie contract in the NFL. Bosworth was all about individual titles and being the highest of anything so he decided that Hollywood would have to wait for the time being.

Educational-wise, Bosworth wasn't as dumb as he tried to look and got good grades in school. Nonetheless, his reputation for being a 'me-me-me' kind of guy was well deserved. While at the UO, he gave himself the nickname, 'The Boz', and looked for publicity and controversy wherever he went. He wore his hair in styles that reflected those desires.

At the end of his second season in college, Bosworth was busted by the NCAA for steroid use. Bosworth claimed the drugs were prescribed by a doctor for injuries that he had sustained while playing football. The NCAA didn't buy it and suspended Bosworth from playing in the Orange Bowl that year. Bosworth was pissed and declared to everyone that would listen that NCAA stood for 'National Communists Against Athletes'. He even had a tee shirt made with those words affixed to it and unveiled the shirt to the crowd and national television audience while standing on the sidelines during the Orange Bowl game.

Coach Barry Switzer was blindsided by the incident and when he saw Bosworth display the tee shirt during the game, he'd had enough. He tossed Bosworth from the football team, and Bosworth's collegiate career was over.

And that's how it came to be that a two-time All-American with a rather large chip on his rather large shoulders entered the supplemental NFL draft.

(The NFL's supplemental draft was designed to give underclassmen, who did not petition the NFL for early entry, but who are ineligible for the up-coming college season, a way to get into the league.)

After he was drafted by Seattle, Bosworth demanded he be allowed to wear his old college uniform number of 44. However, since the NFL prohibited linebackers from wearing numbers in the 40's, his demand was politely refused. So, like the good solider he was, and before he even played a down as a professional, Bosworth sued the NFL for the right to wear number 44. Really, how could they expect him to play without *his* favorite number on his back? *Wah, wah, wah.*

But when the courts ruled against him, Bosworth had no choice but to begrudgingly grace the grid iron with the bourgeois number of 55 on his uniform. When the first game of the regular season at Denver approached, Bosworth announced to the media that he couldn't wait to get his hands on the Broncos' quarterback John Elway's face and rip his lips off. This didn't sit well with some Denver fans and ten thousand of them showed up at Mile High Stadium wearing tee shirts that read, "Ban the Boz".

However, what those fans didn't know at the time was, the tee shirts they were wearing, were made by a company *owned* by Bosworth. We mentioned earlier that he did good in school, didn't we?

Nevertheless, Denver picked apart the Seahawks defense and the Bronco's won 40-17. In a post-game interview, John Elway's lips were still in place and working fine. Later in his first season, The Boz started crowing again, saying he would contain the Raiders' Bo Jackson in a Monday Night Football game against Seattle in the Kingdome. During the game, in a play 'seen round the world 'on television, Jackson took a hand-off in the red zone and knocked the Boz on his butt, dragging him into the end zone for a touchdown. It was reported that after the play was over, Jackson said to the Boz, "Next time we meet, make sure you bring bus fare."

The Raiders won that game 37-14. Jackson was 'held' to 221 rushing yards while scoring just three touchdowns.

With four games left in the regular season, Seattle fans were questioning whether Bosworth was the panacea they had been hoping for. He had played okay so far, but The Boz 'glow' was losing its luster. The team still had a good chance of making the play-offs, but the lost to the Raiders on the Monday Night Football game meant that they would have to win out if they were going to improve on their record from the year before.

CHAPTER FORTY-SIX

During the holidays, Bosworth stopped in at Swannies for a drink and so people could look at him. The bling he wore was as sparkling as the Christmas lights outside. His new Corvette parked just across the street.

The place was about half full as Bosworth walked straight to the bar, stood near an empty stool and waited to order a drink from Swannie. A young man and woman seated to his Bosworth's left were purring over each other and oblivious to his presence. To his right a couple of guys in their late twenties were watching the tube and arguing sports.

The two seemed to have been at the bar for a while.

When Swannie brought Bosworth his drink, he asked him, "Anything else, Boz?" That got the attention of the two guys. They both stopped what they were doing and turned to look to their left. The one farthest away raised his glass and said, "Hey, Boz. How's it going man?"

Bosworth smirked slightly and nodded.

The two guys went back to their drinks and conversation, but now in hushed tones as their topic of discussion became the big man next to them. After a minute or two the same guy looked over and asked Bosworth, "How come you don't wear your old jersey number from college?"

Bosworth took a drink and said out of the side of his mouth, "I wanted to, but the NFL wouldn't let me."

"Really? How come?"

"Some stupid rule. I sued 'em but they still wouldn't let me wear my old number."

The guy took a second to digest what he'd just heard, then; "Wait a minute. You mean you sued the NFL?"

"Yeah."

"Because they wouldn't let you wear your old number?"

Bosworth shot the guy a look. "It wasn't just some old number, it was *my* number, 44."

Guy number one raised his eyebrows and turned to look at guy number two. Looks were being shot all over the place. And then the two guys fell back into a conspiratorial huddle. After a couple of laughs, it was guy number one's turn. He raised his glass and turned back to Bosworth.

"Hey. I remember reading about you owning the company that sold all those 'Bash the Boz' tee shirts. Nice move."

Bosworth was becoming increasingly annoyed. "It wasn't 'bash', it was 'ban'." "Huh?"

"*Ban* the Boz. The shirt said. 'Ban the Boz', not bash. You said bash."

Number one gave it some thought and shook his head. "I think *bash* makes more sense."

Bosworth jaw muscles clenched but he didn't say anything. Number two guy wasn't through. "Did you really sue the NFL?"

About that time Swannie came down the bar and asked if anybody wanted another drink. Bosworth said he'd like one and then added in a big voice, "Hopefully I'll be able to drink this one in peace."

The dialogue was not lost on the two former Boz fans. They grew very quiet and soon went back into their private huddle. After a while they threw down their drinks and stood up to leave. As number one guy left a tip on the bar, he wondered aloud, "What the hell's a Boz worth anyway?" Then he answered his own question. "Nothing compared to a Jackson, ha! We're outta here."

Bosworth got his wish and for the next twenty minutes he enjoyed his drink alone. Then he, too, decided it was time to go. He left a tip for Swannie and strutted out the door. Unfortunately, five minutes later he came bursting back in like he was about to tackle somebody. He went straight to Swannie. "Goddamn it! Somebody just smashed in the windshield on my car!"

Swannie was stunned. "Ah shit, man. I'm sorry to hear that. You want me to call---."

"It was probably those two-little fuck-heads you let in! The ones that were sittin' right here!"

"Okay, okay, settle down, I'll----

"Fuck you, settle down! It wasn't your windshield they bashed!"

Bosworth was pointing his finger at Swannie like he was going to jump across the bar and grab him by the throat. The Boz continued his rant, "And if you think for one minute that *I'm* gonna pay to get my windshield replaced, *you* are one crazy little fucker!"

Swannie blinked once, took a breath, and said, "Well, you know, I think you're right. If I were you, I wouldn't pay for it either."

That quieted Bosworth for a second. But then Swannie said, "If I were you, I'd just buy a whole new car."

"What? The hell you talkin' about?" Bosworth demanded.

Swannie looked serious. "Well, I've heard that windshields on Corvettes can be a bugger to replace. It's hard to get 'em in just right so they don't leak. *I* think you'd be better off just buying a whole new car. Maybe think about a different color this time though, huh?"

Unnoticed by Bosworth, two off-duty cops were sitting nearby, watching and listening in. They were regulars at Swannies and started smiling and nodding as if Swannie was making perfect sense.

Bosworth purpled up. "This is bullshit. What kinda joint you running here, anyway?" One of the cops stood up, "Want us to call the cops, Swannie?"

Swannie just shrugged, "I don't care, wasn't my car that got bashed." Swannie turned and walked away.

Bosworth fumed for a moment and then did an about-face and stormed back outside. A few seconds passed before there was a sound of a powerful engine starting, followed by screeching rubber. The Boz had left the building.

A year and a half later, the Boz left the Seattle Seahawks and professional football as well. The Boz's forced retirement was ostensibly due to a shoulder injury he suffered while playing in a game for Seattle. However, the Seattle Seahawks doctor,

Pierce E. Scraton Jr, who examined Bosworth said, "Brian flunked my physical. In my opinion, he is a twenty-five-year-old with the shoulders of a sixty-year old" (see 'degenerative arthritis').

Bosworth argued that his injury was due to one specific hit and was entitled to all the money in his contract. On the way out the door, Bosworth sued his insurance company, Lloyds of London, for good measure.

Years later, Bosworth was awarded seven million dollars as a result of the lawsuit with LOL.

Bosworth, now free to pursue a career in Hollywood, starred in the movie, *Stone Cold*. However, it was apparent that he didn't use any of his money for acting lessons and the movie was panned. No word yet if Bosworth sued the director.

CHAPTER FORTY-SEVEN

Ellen DeGeneres

Another comedy act that was gaining traction in the 80's was a gal named Ellen DeGeneres. Although Ellen was in her mid-twenties when she played Swannie's, she had been earning her chops since she was a kid. Ellen was born in Metairie, Louisiana, January 26th, 1958. She is of French, English, German, and Irish descent, and grew up making people of all creeds and colors laugh.

And, like many aspiring stand-up comics, she worked at many other jobs along the way. A clerk at J.C. Penny. A bartender and waitress at T.G.I.F.'s, and as a house painter. And, like a lot of her fellow comics, she was able to draw from these work experiences for a laugh. Just the idea of painting a house should make people laugh, right?

Ellen started her stand-up act by working small clubs and coffee shops, no surprise there either, but what did come as a surprise much later in her life, was a letter from the New England Historic Genealogical Society confirming she is the 15th cousin of Catherine, Duchess of Cambridge, aka Kate Middleton, wife of Prince William. Not sure if this relationship is something Ellen can or will use for laughs, but it might be interesting to see how she would describe her Royal relatives, especially that chuckle-head, Prince Charles.

Swannie was beside himself when Jon Fox told him he had signed Ellen. He couldn't wait to meet her and ask her out. Fox, being the fox that he was, warned Ellen about Mr. Swanson and told her of some of his shenanigans when he was with the Mavericks. "Be careful," he told her. "He's quite the jokester himself. You might want to keep him at least arm's length."

When the big night came, Swannie wasn't working, but he was upstairs behind the bar trying to look busy while waiting to meet Ellen. Mostly he was rehearsing clever lines and checking himself out in the mirror. Hair just right. No nose buggers. Practicing his smile. Checking his breath. Winking at himself.

Finally, Ellen walked in alone, went straight to the bar and introduced herself. She was wearing a gray pants suit with a blood red blouse and looked great. Swannie immediately dropped the glass he was drying. 'Shit' was the first word out of his mouth, then; "Oh, hey. Excuse me! Nice to meet you. I'm, ah, Jim. Jim Swanson. But my friends call me Swannie."

Ellen smiled and extended her hand. "Nice to meet you, Sweeny."

"Swannie."

"Huh?"

"Swannie. People call me Swannie."

"That's cute. Why do they call you that?"

Swannie hadn't prepared for the question and what confidence he had mustered up went somewhere else. He fumbled with an answer, "Ah, well, that's because of my name, you know? That's why this place is called Swannies."

Ellen cocked her head and frowned as if she didn't get the connection. She had a wide-eyed look on her face and said, "You could call it "Jimmy's" then too, huh? Because of your name? Or, how about "Jim's Inn"? That has a nice ring to it."

Swannie looked around, wondering if this girl had been hit by a bus recently. He started to have second thoughts about asking her out. He looked back at her and said, "Well, maybe when you get *your* own place, you could call it, 'Degenerates,' or somethin' like that, huh?"

Ellen appeared to think that over for another moment and then winkled her nose. "Nah, that doesn't do anything for me, but thank you anyway, Sweeny."

Now Swannie was sure he wanted some distance from this person. He pointed toward the stairs,

"Well, feel free to use my office downstairs if you need to rehearse or something."

"Rehearse?" Ellen asked, continuing the dumb act. She let the question hang in the air for another beat and watched Swannie squirm. Finally, she smiled and asked, "Whaddya think I've been doing since I walked in here?"

Swannie looked at her and saw the twinkle in her eyes. He stood there a moment, and then it hit him. *Duh!* He'd just been Ellen-ed! (We did mention that Ellen gets a lot of her material while on the job, right?)

At first Swannie was pissed, but he quickly regrouped, thinking how this might still work out in a date with her. "Okay, okay, you got me," he said sheepishly, raising his hands in surrender. "But now you owe me. How 'bout joining me for a drink after your act? I could show you around Seattle a little?"

Ellen politely declined, saying she was sorry but she was in a relationship. Swannie countered with a couple of clever witticisms insinuating that going out with him would trump anything she had going at the time. He even apologized for the 'degenerates' comment.

When Ellen held her ground Swannie finally had to give in. Love would just have to wait...for the time being anyway. Swannie walked her over to the stairs and wished her well. "Break a leg," he said. "Not here on the stairs of course, but you know, break a leg, heh, heh."

Ellen laughed. "I'll try." She took one step and turned around "And thanks for letting me warm up on you...Sweeny."

The Swandog went back to the bar, made himself a drink, and stood there looking at it.

Sweeny? Really?

He didn't know it then, but love *was* waiting, and it was just down the block.

(photo: Jim Swanson)

Rusty 'likes' Ellen

CHAPTER FORTY-EIGHT

Swannie was still looking at his drink when Dave Henderson walked in and grabbed a seat at the bar. He knew right away that something was up, or in this case, down.

Swannie never spent much time just looking at a drink. Normally the word 'drink' was a verb and implied action to him, or as Webster defines it; *to take (a liquid) in the mouth and swallow.*

"What's so funny?" Henderson asked, sarcastically.

Swannie finally took a slug from his drink (noun) and said, "Hopefully the gal that was just here, Ellen. She's on stage tonight."

"Ellen? Ellen who?"

"You got that right," Swannie said. "I don't know why Fox signed her. She kept calling me, *Sw-e-e-e-ny.'!* She's probably not gonna last too long as a comedian. I just hope she doesn't bomb tonight."

Henderson nodded his head. "Okay. I can see what's happening here. As your love counselor, I advise you to do two things immediately; okay, make that three things, first; forget about Ellen 'what's-her-name', second; finish your drink, and then third, you and me boogie down to Pier 70. Their house band is really good. They play some Beatles songs better'n the Beatles do. Should be some booty down there."

Swannie ticked his instructions off. "Ellen who?" And then he drained his glass, slammed it down on the bar, and smiled at Henderson. "Let's boogie."

Pier 70 was about a five-minute ride from Swannies. It was a trendy spot in the 80's and usually drew a nice crowd. When Henderson and Swannie walked into the place, it was about three-quarters full, equal part girls and boys. Apparently, the band had been on a break but a few of the musicians were just returning to the stage, laughing about something and fiddling with their instruments.

Swannie and Henderson grabbed a two-seater table near the dance floor, ordered drinks from a passing waitress, and casually eye-balled the talent around them.

"Nice assortment tonight," Henderson observed.

"No shit." Swannie agreed.

"You over her yet?"

"Over who?"

"Atta boy."

Swannie had noticed a girl sitting with two couples across the dance floor. She was wearing a red sweater, cowboy boots, and faded blue jeans. Her dishwater blonde hair was mussed perfectly and held together with a black ribbon. She seemed to be having a good time with the people at the table, like she was with old friends. When she smiled, dimples book-ended a dazzlingly white smile. She instantly reminded Swannie of 'ol what's-her-name'.

On stage, the musicians finished tuning-up and the front man took the mike. As he reintroduced each member of the band, people started getting up, getting ready to get down.

When Swannie saw the girl beginning to get loose in her seat, he knew he had to get to her table before anybody else did. The Swandog was mesmerized and on a mission. He was halfway to her table when the band kicked in.

...Well, she was just seventeen. You know what I mean...And the way she looked, was way beyond compare...

Swannie was three steps from her table when a long-haired, hippie-looking dude, arrived at the target area just ahead of him. Hippie-dude smiled at the girl and gestured toward the dance floor. She stood up. Swannie had a split-second decision to make; either stop right where he was and go back to his table, or, keep on walking past her as if he were going somewhere else anyway.

...How could I dance with another, When I saw her standing there.

168

At the last moment Swannie's decision making part of his brain short-circuited and his forward momentum carried him to the girl's table. He was in an awkward situation for a second before his tongue took over. "Hi, Honey. Gee, sorry I'm late." Swannie smiled and waved at the two couples, saying loudly over the band. "Hey guys! Good to see you." He gave them a thumbs-up to them for good measure.

...Well, she looked at me...And, I, I could see...That before too long... I'd fall in love with her...

Hippie-dude looked at Swannie, a glazed, stoned look, "ah...who are you, man?" Swannie leaned in close. "Me? I'm Jim Swanson. Nice to meet you." He reached out, picked up the guy's limp hand, pumped it once, and let it drop. Then he looked at the girl. "And this is here's my fiancé...Lois."

Swannie looked at the girl and motioned toward the dance floor. She had a funny look on her face, and he couldn't tell whether she was going to blow his cover or not. Finally, she smiled and started walking toward the dance floor. She hesitated briefly as she passed by Swannie and asked under her breath, "Lois?"

...Well my heart went boom, when I crossed that room, and I held her hand in miiiiine...

Swannie followed the girl to the middle of the dance floor and because the music was a little too loud for casual conversation, they just got with it.

...Whoa, we danced thru the night, and held each other tight...and before too long, I fell in love with her...

When the song ended, they stayed in the middle of the floor. "You're a good dancer," Swannie said. She smiled and answered, "You're not." She let Swannie sweat a little before she said..."but, I like your moves. You may have saved me back there. Did I hear you say your name was Jim?"

"Yeah, Jim Swanson." Swannie was having a hard time concentrating. Her blue eyes were penetrating and he could smell her perfume. "...but, you know, my friends call me, Sweeny."

"Sweeny?"

"I mean, Swannie."

She looked at him skeptically, "Which is it? Sweeny or Swannie?"

"Do you know Ellen DeGeneres?"

"No. Should I?"

The music started up again and Swannie was saved.

When the next song was over, they were walking back to her table when she stopped abruptly. "Wait a minute. If we're engaged, shouldn't I be wearing a ring?"

Without hesitation, or taking his eyes off of her, Swannie pulled his class ring off and handed it to her.

First, she tried putting it on the proper finger, but the ring was much too big. Then she tried the other fingers with the same results. Finally, she slipped it on her thumb where it fit nicely. She held it at arm's length and admired it for a moment. "Okay. I can't wait to show my friends. By the way, my name is Debbie."

When they got to her table she announced, "Guys, I'd like you to meet Sweeny---"

"---Swannie."

"Sweeny, Swannie, whatever." She laughed and proudly held up her left thumb for all to see. "Look. We're engaged."

One month later, Swannie replaced his class ring with the real thing.

...And I'll never dance with another, Since I saw her standing there.

CHAPTER FORTY-NINE

Debbie was twenty-six years old, divorced with two kids, a six-year old boy named Gabriel and a four-year old girl named Ashley. The fact that Debbie had two kids didn't faze Swannie at all. "When we get married, I get to be a father without changing single diaper!" Swannie even thought Debbie's ex-husband was a good guy. The first time he met him he said to him, "Thanks for doing all the dirty work. Rest assured I will treat the kids just like they were our own."

He must have been a good guy for not punching Swannie in the nose right then and there.

Debbie also had a cute, younger sister named Renee, who practically gushed over Swannie the first day she met him. "If the comedians you hire are as half as funny as you, you got it made. You're a hoot!"

As Debbie and Swannie dated hot and heavy, Renee didn't mind babysitting for her sister. She loved Debbie's kids and thought Swannie was a rock star. "Sis, you better hang on to this guy. He knows *every*body."

At first their dates were typical for people their age. Dinner, a movie, some dancing at the local clubs. If the there was a sporting event in town, Swannie could always score tickets if Debbie wanted to go, which was most of the time. It seemed like wherever Swannie wanted to go or whatever he wanted to do; she was up for it. She was the girl in Waylon Jennings' song, *She's a Good-Hearted Woman, Lovin' a Good-Timin' Man.* Of course, most people in their twenties don't need an excuse to party-hearty but hanging with Swannie meant hanging with some pretty fashionable folk. In May of 1985, a survey by the *Seattle Times* named Swannies the second-best sports bar in the Greater Seattle Area. Beating out such establishments as DiMaggio's, Bogeys, and F.X. McCrory's. Peter's Inn came in a distant 13th.

When told of his award Swannie was pissed, "Whaddya mean *second* best? Did God open up a sports bar that I'm not aware of? Ask Yogi Berra which joint he likes best. Or how 'bout Huey Lewis, Bob Uecker, Chris Berman, hell, those are just a few of the guys that showed up at my place. Not to mention half of the American Baseball League. The list goes on, you know?"

The list indeed did go on, if you were anybody at all and you came into Swannies, it was deemed an honor if you would step behind the bar and serve up cocktails as a guest bartender.

Before he met Debbie, Swannie was consumed with his club. It was his lifeblood. He was always looking for ways to improve on things, making sure everything was just right and everyone was having a good time. He never sucked up to anybody but never shied away from having a drink or two with a celeb either. He stayed late just about every night. Partying after hours. Schmoozing. His mantra was, "Let it happen, Capt'n!"

Then, after six months of dating Debbie, Swannie was, well, still consumed with his club. After a while, instead of going out on a date, he began asking Debbie to meet him at his bar. "We're a little short-handed tonight. I better go in to work," Swannie would say. Then, "Why don't you meet me there? We'll have just as much fun there as anywhere else anyway."

Like a good trooper, Debbie would come in and sit at the bar. Swannie kept her entertained by introducing her to everyone. "Honey, I'd like you to meet Jack Sikma. He's plays center for the Sonic's...Sweetie, this is Reggie McKenzie, he's the Seahawks' left tackle...Debbie, this is Bill Maher, he's playing here tonight. We'll go downstairs and catch some of his act later. He's one funny dude, I'll tell ya."

At first Debbie enjoyed the action at Swannies. There was never a dull moment. But after a while she began to wonder where their romance was headed. She didn't know if she enjoyed sharing her man with everyone else. It was beginning to seem like they didn't spend much time alone anymore.

So, when Swannie asked her to marry him, she surprised everyone, including herself by saying yes. She worked it out with her ex that once she was married, her son, Gabriel would stay with his father while her daughter, Ashley, would live with Debbie and Swannie.

By this time Debbie knew she was taking a big chance because of Swannie's lifestyle, but she loved him and had a vague notion that marriage might just be what this freewheeling bachelor needed in his life.

(photo: Rod Long)

Hanging with the Big Boys: Reggie McKenzie,
Swannie, and Larry Csonka

CHAPTER FIFTY

The two were married in Seattle on April 4th, 1981. They moved into an apartment in Leschi, on Lake Washington, with great expectations of living happily-ever-after.

Debbie was hoping to go to Hawaii on a honeymoon right away, but Swannie begged off. "I can't really afford to take time off right now, hon, you know, too much going on at the club. Besides, baseball season's just getting started. Let's wait til things slow down and then I'll take my honey to the moon if you want, okay?"

Debbie was disappointed but not surprised. She tried subtly to change his mind. "I don't want the moon, dear, just a few days with you on a warm beach, that's all."

Swannie smiled and kissed her. "Ah, that's my girl. I knew you'd understand."

Debbie just shook her head, and then like the amiable woman she was, she acquiesced to yet another one of Swannie's requests.

Nine months later, as baseball season came and went, the Swanson's had yet to leave town for a honeymoon. "Soon as I can find some more help, we'll get outta here", Swannie would say.

Debbie countered by saying her sister would make a fine waitress, "Why don't you hire her? She needs work and you say you need to hire someone, right?"

Swannie countered that counter by caving completely and hiring Renee. "We'll have to wait and see how she works out though."

As it turned out, Renee worked out just fine. She quickly picked up the nuances of the job and loved working the busy shifts. She got along with everyone and made great tips. Swannie couldn't have asked for a better employee.

Naturally as time went by, Renee relayed all of this to her sister. Renee in her excitement would also mention what a good boss Swannie was and how much fun he was to be around. Unwittingly, she would repeat some of the raunchy repartee that went on at Swannies, none of which would fly in today's politically on-guard correctness. Of course, by now you probably realize that nothing about Swannie is, was, or ever will be, politically correct.

Renee would also say things like, "Boy, Swannie's place has gotta be making a ton of money with all the people that hang out there. You must be really proud of him, huh Sis?"

Then Debbie would say things like, "I suppose so, but you'd think we could afford to take a honeymoon by now. Doesn't have to be Hawaii, just someplace where we could relax and be together."

"You guys getting along okay?" Renee asked. "Is there trouble in paradise?"

"Oh, we're fine. I just wish he would work normal hours like most people. He doesn't usually get home till three or four in the morning and when he does get home, he's wobbly and smells like an ashtray. Then he sleeps till late in the afternoon."

"Why don't you come to the club like you used to? You guys always had fun." Debbie looked at her sister long and hard. "Well, for one thing, I don't have a babysitter like I used to."

(photo: Sue Swanson)

All smiles on Wedding Day; Swannie with his Mom and Debbie

CHAPTER FIFTY-ONE

In the mid-eighties, Huey Lewis and the News were rocking the musical landscape with hits like, "I Want a New Drug", and, "If This Is It." Swannie was a big fan so when he heard that Huey and Co. would be playing at the Puyallup Fair to promote their new album, 'Sports,' he asked one of his managers to go with him to watch the band play. As it turned out, his manager was a friend of a friend who got them backstage passes.

The show was packed but Swannie and his manager did get backstage and in between sets were introduced to Mr. Lewis. Swannie immediately started playing air guitar and singing, "The heart of Rock and Roll." Lewis seemed to get a kick out of Swannie and playfully covered his ears. Before the concert was over, Swannie handed Lewis one of his business cards and invited him to come by Swannies if he ever got the chance.

A week later, on a beautiful fall day, and much to Swannie's delight, Huey Lewis and his keyboard player, Sean Hopper, did pop by. It was about three o'clock in the afternoon, the lunch crowd was mostly gone, and the happy hour people hadn't arrived yet. Swannie was behind the bar talking with Dave Henderson when the two musicians walked through the open door at Swannies.

"Boy, you really pack 'em in here don't you?" Lewis said as he looked around to the mostly deserted place.

Swannie looked up from what he was doing. "Hey Man! Glad you could make it. Come on in, pull up a stool."

The two did as instructed and Swannie introduced them to Henderson. Lewis was a sports fan and knew Henderson was playing for the Mariners. "Got another October off, I see," he said, as he shook Henderson's hand. Henderson was a fan of Lewis and knew his history too. "Just like your Giants?"

There was some more good-natured jiving and soon drinks were ordered. Swannie gave Hopper and Lewis a quick tour of the place and then returned to the bar. That's when Lewis spotted the piano. "Why is that piano up there?"

"What piano?" Swannie answered with a straight face.

"Oh, that's right. This place is a comedy club. You're not the headliner, are you?" Lewis asked.

Hopper was curious about the piano too. "I want to know how in the hell you got it up there? It looks like a Steinway. Is it in tune?"

"It was when we put it up there," Swannie said. "You're welcome to play it if you want."

"Yeah, right. How would I get up there? Stand on the bar and hop up?"

"Well, there is an easier way to get up there," Swannie said. "But that's how Dave does it, Mr. Hopper. He just hops up there. Right, Dave?"

All eyes were now on Henderson who was looking a little coy.

Nobody said anything until Lewis asked, "Well, Dave? You want to show us how you do it?"

Henderson smiled, got up and pushed his stool away. He looked at Hopper. "I tell you what, if I can stand right here, flat-footed, and jump up on to the top of this bar, will you climb up there and play a tune for us?"

Hopper laughed. "I don't know what the catch is, but if you can jump straight up from where you're standing, and land on the bar, I'll kiss your ass and give you an hour to draw a crowd. Then I'll get up there and play all afternoon."

Henderson's smile got even wider and he looked at Swannie. Swannie smiled back and cleared an area on the bar. "You heard the man, Dave. Do your thing."

Henderson didn't hesitate. He kicked off his shoes, took three quick breaths, squatted, and then shot straight up and landed on the bar like an eagle.

Lewis and Hopper were stunned for a moment. Then they both started laughing and applauding.

About that time, two guys that were regulars in Swannies came in. Although their eyes hadn't completely adjusted from coming in out of the sunshine, one of them squinted and said loudly, "How much you win this time, Dave?" They'd seen Henderson do his amazing stunt many times. When Henderson jumped down off of the bar and explained the wager, one of the guys said, "Okay, that's cool. But maybe you got suckered this time, Dave." Obliviously the guy hadn't recognized Lewis or Hopper yet. "Do you know if this man can even play the piano?" Lewis looked at Hopper. "Well, Sean? You made the bet. You wanna show the man if you can play or not?"

Swannie helped Hopper make his decision by walking to the one end of the bar and pulling back a black curtain that concealed a short, steel rung ladder that led up to the platform that the piano was on. Hopper smiled, got off his bar stool and walked over to the ladder. As he was climbing up, he asked over his shoulder, "Anything in particular you guys wanna hear?"

The two regulars were just sitting down at a table, and one answered, "How 'bout 'Chopsticks' in B minor?" The two laughed as if they were in cahoots about something.

Hopper made his way to the piano, pulled up the bench seat and made a few stabs at different keys. The two regulars were feeling pretty smug...right up until Hopper coughed, leaned forward, and suddenly launched into a tune that literally and figuratively rocked the bar.

The acoustics surrounding the piano were awesome. As Hopper played, a few more customers drifted in and listened. When Hopper finally finished the song, all hands were clapping, including from some people that were outside on the sidewalk, looking in.

Sensing what was happening, Lewis stood up and caught Hopper's eye. Lewis pulled a mouth harp out of his shirt pocket, pointed it at his keyboardist and said, "This sure beats working for a living doesn't it?"

Taking his cue, Hopper wasted no time and jumped into the song, 'Working for a Living.' In was immediately clear that these two musicians knew each other's moves completely and loved what they were doing.

Lewis and Hopper pumped out more songs and about an hour later, when they finally stopped playing, Swannies was packed inside and out.

(photo: Rod Long)

Hangin' with Huey

CHAPTER FIFTY-TWO

One afternoon after Swannie got out of bed, he scratched his way to the kitchen for his wake-up coffee. Debbie was there waiting for him and handed him his cup. She waited for him to sit down and take a sip before she delivered the news that she was pregnant. "You're what?" Swannie asked after he coughed and wiped coffee from his nose.

"I'm pregnant. You know, P.G? Preggers? With child? One-in-the-oven?"

He looked at her in total disbelief. "Wait a minute. Cut the shit. You're telling me that you're *preg-nant*?"

"That's exactly what I'm telling you." "You can't be pregnant."

"And, why not?"

"Well, you know, we agreed not to. Get pregnant that is." "Well, hotshot, I am. Pregnant, that is."

"Are you sure?"

Debbie shook her head. "Why do men always ask that? Are you *sure*? Of course, I'm sure, or I wouldn't have said anything."

Swannie sat there stunned for a second or two trying to digest the news. Finally, he asked, "Are you sure it's yours?"

Debbie glared at her husband. He *was* kidding right? Swannie offered a weak smile which didn't help. That's when Debbie teared up and started to cry. "Damn you! I thought you would be happy!" She got up and started to walk out of the kitchen.

Swannie was smart enough to get up and intercept her. He hugged her and said, "Wait a minute, honey. I was just kidding! Of course, I'm happy. I love you. I hope we're having twins!"

Debbie softened but still looked dubiously at her husband. Swannie was in a tough spot and he knew it. There was only one thing left he could do. Stepping away he broke into his soft-shoe-tap dance, Irish sort of a jig that never failed to produce a smile. For good measure he crooned; "How I love you, how I love you...my dear old Mammy."

It was pure cornball but it worked...for a while anyway. Debbie smiled, shook her head and sat back down at the table. Swannie reached out and took her hand. "It'll be a boy, right?"

CHAPTER FIFTY-THREE

It was a boy. All 9 pounds, nine ounces of him. Tanner
James Swanson was born on August 31, 1982. Debbie and
Tanner were both healthy and to hear it from the proud Swandog,
Tanner didn't even cry when he entered this world...he laughed
instead.

Probably because the first thing he saw was his father trying
to dance.

To say that Swannie was happy would be an understatement.
The first night after Tanner was born, Swannie went through all
the hallways in his apartment, drink in hand, ringing doorbells,
pounding on doors, letting everyone know, "It's a boy! It's a
boy!"

The next night at work was more of the same. The Boston
Red Sox happened to be in town and after the game the joint was
jumping. Swannie carried a Polaroid picture of his new son and
proudly showed every living soul around him, which included
Boston's young pitching phenom, Roger Clemens, who happened
to be outside at the time, throwing lemons across the street.

Swannie drank so much that night the cops that were at the
club gave him a ride home. The next day, he was hungover and
feeling a little sheepish about getting a ride home in a patrol car.
Debbie was thankful that he made it home safely and assumed it
wouldn't happen again. Boy was she wrong

CHAPTER FIFTY-FOUR

Cheech and Chong

While Debbie spent most of her time at home doing all the good things mothers do so their children can grow up healthy and strong, Swannie spent most of his time at the club doing all the things he could do to keep his establishment strong and healthy. After all, he had another mouth to feed now.

John Fox was keeping his word by supplying Swannie with funny people. Unlike Seinfeld and DeGeneres who were just getting started in the funny business, Cheech and Chong were already established stars when they played Swannies. In fact, they had been together for so long they were about to breakup.

Tommy B. Kin Chong first met Richard 'Cheech' Marin in a topless bar in Vancouver, Canada. It was in the mid 60's and although both men had their shirts on at the time, Chong thought Cheech looked like a "biker-hippie-weightlifter-escapee from Mongolia."

Cheech was born on July 13, 1946, in East Los Angeles, where he lived most of the time before escaping the U.S draft by fleeing to Canada. Cheech had been motivated to do so after hearing a speech given by Muhammad Ali at the San Fernando Valley State College (now Cal State University). Cheech of course was stoned at the time and when Ali said, "I ain't got no quarrel with them Vietcong," it made perfect sense to Cheech, so, off he fled (He later got Ali to autograph his draft card before he burned it).

Tommy Chong was born in Edmonton, Alberta, Canada on May 24th, 1938. Although he had Irish and Chinese blood in him, Chong was a Canadian which meant he didn't have to flee anywhere, unless he just wanted to get away from polite people.

When Chong's family moved to Vancouver, they opened a strip joint and improv comedy club where Chong would eventually meet Cheech. Chong was a musician by then, so he often played guitar at the club. Family-owned-and-operated at its best, no?

With a place to work out a routine, it didn't take Cheech and Chong long to get their own stand-up act rolling. They added to their success in 1978 when they made the transition to the big screen with the cult stoner hit, "Up in Smoke". The movie was produced on a low budget but took in more than one hundred million dollars at the box office. It also established Cheech and Chong as the official symbols of the marijuana culture.

When Jon Fox told Swannie that he'd lined up Cheech and Chong for a couple of nights, Swannie thought that was cool. He knew that C&C had many films and albums to their credit and were seemingly at the top of their game. Swannie was never a big pot smoker, or taker of drugs, even during his Portland's Maverick daze, but if folks wanted to get stoned and act a little silly, he was alright with that. Swannie even thought that if the opportunity presented itself, he would probably have a toke or two with Cheech and Chong. Maybe after the show. In the alley.

Swannie didn't know it at the time, but the opportunity was about to present itself, just not the way he had in mind.

It wasn't unusual for entertainers or comedy acts at Swannies to enter through a back door off of the alley. If they needed to go over their routine or relax before they went on stage, Swannie's office was available for them. Often, comedians stayed there until they were called onstage. Such was the case with Cheech and Chong the night in question.

At 7:30 pm, while C&C were in his office, Swannie was upstairs working the bar and looking forward to a busy and lucrative night. Usually when an opening act was introduced, or the act was especially funny, Swannie could feel and hear the reaction from the crowd below. As time passed, Swannie had yet to hear anything. Finally, he went downstairs and asked his manager why the act hadn't started yet. The manager said he'd knocked on the office door and called but didn't get a response.

He also said that the audience kept looking over their shoulders toward the office and was getting impatient.

Swannie walked back to the office door and opened it. Immediately a huge cloud of smoke came pouring out and Swannie backed away coughing. A second or two passed before Cheech and then Chong came slowly out of the door looking around as if they didn't know where they were. They were clearly stoned to the bone and Swannie was pissed. He had heard the two arguing and knew it wasn't part of their act. But the crowd didn't know that, and they suddenly started applauding like crazy As the two comedians made their way to the stage, Swannie made an exaggerated motion of sucking in the smoke around him as if he were taking a hit. He held his breath for a moment, then let it out, made a 'happy face', turned and went back upstairs.

Unfortunately, Cheech and Chong had been arguing that night. Shortly after playing Swannies, the two broke up. The split was contentious for a couple of years but in 1992 the two worked together voicing characters in an animated film called *FernGully*. This led to more reconciliation and soon they began working together again on other, *ahem*, joint ventures.

CHAPTER FIFTY-FIVE

Two years after Tanner Swanson was born, Debbie delivered the news that she was pregnant again. Swannie took the tidings as he had before. "Wait a minute, are you sure? I thought we agreed not to have any more children!"

Debbie was disappointed *again* at his reaction and started crying. Swannie quickly realized he had *again* said the wrong thing and tried another lame attempt at humor, always his out-card.

"Whaddya think's causing these kids?"

Debbie stifled her sobs long enough to answer, "That's a good question, since you're not around that much."

This time the Swanson's had a beautiful baby girl they named Lily. And again, Swannie celebrated to the max, which led to another ride home in a patrol car. Debbie gave her husband another pass on the ride home because of the joyous occasion, but a year later when the cops began giving Swannie a ride home on a regular basis she had a come-to Jesus meeting with her husband. "If you want to save this marriage you better get your drinking under control. And if you want to save yourself, you'll quit smoking too."

Some people might think Debbie was being a nag, but far from it. Debbie was just trying to do the tough-love thing to keep her family intact. Except for the smoking part, Swannie took her words to heart and actually quit drinking. For a while anyway.

CHAPTER FIFTY-SIX

It must be said that throughout his life, Swannie was, and is, color blind. It never mattered to him what race you were as long as it was human. He treated everyone the same. His parents most likely had something to do with that and it served him well, not only in life in general, but in professional sports and the entertainment business too.

As Swannies reputation as a comedy underground grew, comedians from far and wide continually showed up to play there. Male, female, short, tall, fat, thin, black, white, brown and in between. It was an eclectic group for sure, but they all shared something in common; they all loved playing at Swannies. It wa a happy place and the crowds were usually receptive. The comic were appreciative of this of course which made their jobs easier. Most of them were comfortable and loose. Naturally they still had to be funny, but everyone knows that if you have the crowd behind you, it's easier to hit one out of the park.

Swannie was always eager to help local comics too and held an open mic every Monday night. Many of the wanna-be's that showed up had obviously been encouraged by their relatives or friends. "You're a funny sum-bitch. Get up there. We'll clap like hell." Other comics were somewhat seasoned and were just honing their skills. Some were driven by a natural desire and curiosity they couldn't explain.

Such was the case for Seattle resident Rod Long. He came to Swannies one Monday night with a couple of friends to relax and have a good time. Long was a professional photographer of fine arts and had collaborated with notables such as Hollywood's glamour photographer, George Harrell, New York Time's, Micha Bar Am and Vanity Fair's cover shooter, Neal Barr. Long also held a degree in motion Picture Production from Brooks Institute of Photography and a degree in journalism from Seattle University. He wrote a column for Peterson's *Photo Graphic Magazine* and had over two million readers. In other words, the man already had a lot going for him. He wasn't looking for another job.

But, as the night rolled along, and the liquor flowed, Long's friends encouraged him to get up on stage and grab the mic. "You're a writer. You've written some funny shit. Why not comedy? You need more on your current resume, don't you, Rod?"

Finally, after one drink and one dare too many, Long got up and took center stage. He was a little nervous at first but then started talking about something that was dear to him and probably those in the audience; sports. He began with how much money professional athletes were making and who they hired to carry their wallets. He talked about how specialized some sports were becoming and did a funny piece about golfers and the entourage they hired to travel with them; a trainer, coach, caddie, secretary, photographer, a psychic, financial adviser, and a hair stylist.

He brought up Edgar Martinez who was the Mariners designated hitter. He knew that Edgar was beloved in Seattle and wisely gave him kudos for his career, but he made fun of the nature of a designated hitter. "You hit; you sit. You hit; you sit. What's with that?

"And where do designated hitters go for work after retiring from baseball? Demolition crews specializing in brick buildings? Pest control, Rats B Gone?"

Long, who is black, did a spot-on imitation of Muhammad Ali; "Float like a butterfly, sting like a bee. I be the designated hitter, you be the hittee."

When Long finished his bit and walked off the stage to a rousing ovation, he was hooked and his life was changed forever. Swannie, who was the same age as Long, immediately encouraged him to come back and play his venue again.

Long would always have a passion for writing and photography but, now he had another fuel cell to feed off of. Plus, being funny can be a lot of fun.

Not everyone that chooses to become a comedian will go on to have careers like Seinfeld or DeGeneres, and most comics know that. Sometimes its luck, bad or good, that determine how big the bank account becomes. But as most of us know, success and happiness are relative. Even the rich get the flu.

The best thing that most of us can do is follow that old adage that says; "Find something you love to do and you'll never work a day in your life."

That certainly applied to Rod Long. He formed a great relationship with Swannie and began writing jokes and working out different bits. He played Swannies often and soon was making money at stand-up and loving it. He began playing all around Seattle and flying to L.A. for gigs.

Long would go on to win the 1987 Seattle International Comedy Competition and in 1998 won 'Emerald City's Funniest Person' contest. Along the way he opened for acts like Ray Charles, Lou Rawls, The Temptations, Smokey Robinson, Eartha Kitt and yes, he even opened for that Seinfeld fellow.

As of this writing, Long has been doing comedy for almost forty years and has appeared all over the globe. His sideburns are showing some silver and he is at an age where most folks think about retirement. But not Mr. Long. He has most recently been working his trade on the seven seas entertaining folks on cruise ships.

Did I say *working*? Hardly. Rod Long is a happy man and to this day he will tell you that he owes much of that happiness to Jim Swanson, aka, Swannie, for encouraging him to pursue a career in what he loves most, and that's the funny business.

(photo: Terry Cubbins)

Swannie with friend and comic, Rod Long

CHAPTER FIFTY-SEVEN

Somewhere along the line, Swannie had remembered what it was that he had studied in college; Business Administration and Advertising. One of his earlier attempts at advertising came when he hung a neon sign in a window which read, "Sorry. We're Open."

Originally the signs outside and above the entry of Swannies announced the address, '222,' along with, 'Sports...Food...Music'.

When Swannie changed from music to comedy, he had to change the word 'Music' to 'Comedy.' Just before he had his new soft opening, Swannie hired a photographer to take a picture of a group of people outside of his club with the purpose of posting the picture in the local papers to coincide with the new opening. It was a nice sunny day for the photo op and the shoot went well. Swannie sent the photo to the local paper and the picture was dutifully posted as instructed.

Problem was the letters, 'R' and 'S' in the word 'SPORTS,' were mysteriously missing when the photo was taken. Unfortunately, nobody caught the mistake (?) until after the paper came out with the picture. The signs read; "222...SPOT...T...FOOD...COMEDY."

Another example of Swannie's adventures in advertising came when he bought an un-limited hydroplane with the intent of racing it in Seattle's annual Seafair Race on Lake Washington. Seattle has a long history and love affair with the 'Thunder Boats,' and Swannie saw an opportunity to take advantage of the situation. Swannie repainted the hydroplane in a nice combo of rust and yellow to go with his name and logo on the tail fin. He hired a driver by the name of Jack Clark, who had experience racing unlimiteds, but Swannie felt the need to tell him, "Just remember, all the turns are to the left." Swannie and Debbie proudly rode with the boat that year in the Seafair Parade.

All sea trials went well and everything looked good... until race day. When it came time for Swannie's heat, Clark crawled into the cockpit, started the once powerful piston-driven engine and slowly idled the boat away from the dock. Swannie and a group of well-wishers stood nearby and shouted encouragement. Just has Clark applied some throttle, the engine coughed once, blew a perfect smoke ring with the exhaust, and died. Dead in the water, never to regain consciousness. Swannie's involvement with Unlimited Hydroplane Racing was over.

Later, Swannie tried to look on the bright side, "At least we finished first in the parade."

(photo: Sue Swanson)

Friends of Swannie (in blue vest), posing before soft re-opening.

If you're looking for Spotty Food, this is the place!

(photo: Sue Swanson)

Swannie's hydro inching away from the dock

One spring day, 'Jomo', a friend and owner of the nearby Central Saloon, wandered up to Swannies to hang out and talk about promotional ideas for their businesses. It was early in the afternoon and business was slow. Swannie and Jomo sat at corner table sipping non-alcoholic beer and watching ESPN on TV.

They were discussing different promotional ideas for their bars when Dave Valle's face appeared on the TV. Valle was a catcher for the Seattle Mariners and was being interviewed about the big-dollar contract extension he had just received from the M's. At the time, Valle's batting average was below .200 and one of the talking heads for ESPN asked Valle if he thought he deserved the bonus money.

"Of course, I do," Valle explained. "They aren't paying me to *hit,* they're paying me to *catch.*"

When Swannie heard that, he exploded from his chair. "What a bunch of crap! How do you like that guy? Saying they aren't paying him to hit!"

When Jomo didn't say anything, Swannie said, "I could understand it if he was a winy-ass pitcher, but he's a catcher for Christ's sake's!" He looked at Jomo. "Can you imagine Yogi Berra or Johnny Bench saying something like that? They don't pay me to hit! Hell no," Swannie said, looking back to the TV. "I don't get it. He gets all that dough and he can't hit his way out of a paper bag."

"Yeah, well he's hitting better than us," Jomo said. "We can't even come up with a good promotion idea."

Swannie shot back. "Bullshit. He hits a buck seventy-five and he gets a raise? I'm tellin' you that's just not ...'

Swannie stopped talking for a second. Then, "Whoa! Wait a minute. That's it! That's it! We got it!"

Jomo looked at his friend. "Got what?"

Swannie sat back down. "Our promo! Listen. How 'bout we serve drink specials based on Valle's batting average?"

"What the hell you talking about?" Jomo asked.

Swannie eyes lit up. "Sure. That's it! Let's say Valle is hitting one-seventy or something. Okay? So, when the Mariners are in town, that's what we'll charge for drinks on game night. A dollar seventy! If his average goes down, the price goes down. If he gets a hit or two, the price goes up accordingly! Whaddya think?"

Jomo smiled and nodded. "You might have something there."

"You damn right I do," Swannie said. "This could be big!"

Jomo kept nodding but slowly looked away as if deep in thought. "What?" Swannie asked. "What's that look for?"

"Well, what about Valle?" Jomo asked. "Whaddya think his reaction will be to this?" "Who gives a shit?" Swannie said, "Valle's got his bonus. And who knows, maybe his batting average will go up because of this?"

"What if he sues or something?"

"Let him. That's what lawyers are for. Besides, imagine the publicity it'd generate if he did sue. We could put signs in our windows; call it, 'Death Valle Days'. I'm telling you; Bing Russell could really appreciate something like this!"

Jomo, still skeptical: "Valle's a big guy. What if he comes into your place looking for you?"

Swannie laughed hard. "If he comes here looking for me, I'll just take one of the bats off the wall and hand it to him. Valle can't hit shit with a bat in his hands you know."

As it turned out, the idea caught on in a big way. After Swannie displayed his drink special on his windows along with Valle's current batting average, 'Death Valle Daze' and 'See you at Swannies!' signs started appearing in The Kingdome during Mariner games.

More fans started coming in after ball games talking about how Valle did that night. Local papers picked up the buzz and mentioned it in their sports sections. Even *Sports Illustrated* got wind of it and did a short piece on it. The publicity was tremendous and Swannie rolled right with it.

The promotion and fun continued for about three weeks before Swannie got a call from Alvin Davis, the Mariners first baseman and designated hitter. Davis, well respected by fans and players, was calling as the designated speaker in behave of Dave Valle. According to Davis, Valle was getting more and more uncomfortable with Swannie's promotion and the notoriety that came with it.

Davis explained that Valle didn't frequent bars, which by itself wasn't a big thing, but that Valle was getting edgy being identified with one. Davis went on to say that Valle was a good family man and that he harbored no ill will toward Swannie or his establishment.

Swannie listened patiently for Davis to ask the question that he knew was coming;

You think you could find it in your good nature to cease and desist with the promo?

As Davis continued to plead his case, Swannie began thinking of how to say no to Davis. *Business is business, right? Good business too, by the way! Tell Valle to hit better and maybe I'll consider pulling the promo.*

But, by the time Davis wrapped up his case, Swannie found himself wondering how he could say no to the man. Here's a guy who reached base in forty-seven straight games to start his Major League career! He made the All-Star game in his first year! Was voted American League's Rookie of the Year by hitting .284 with twenty-seven home runs and 116 RBI and then named the Mariner's MVP.!!

Plus, he was a nice guy.

So it was, Death Valle Days came to an end. Swannie acquiesced to Davis' request and pulled the plug on his brilliant marketing idea.

In the end, Swannie figured he may have lost some business, but he gained a couple of more friends. And Valle? His batting average began to climb, of course.

(photo: Phil Webber, Seattle P-I)

Swannie and Jomo during Death Valle Days

CHAPTER FIFTY-EIGHT

Steve Palermo was another Major League umpire who liked to hang at Swannies. He took special delight in serving as guest bartender, sometimes demanding well-known athletes like Mariners' Ken Griffey Jr. or Edgar Martinez for their I.D.'s before he would serve them.

Palermo started his career in 1971 and was well respected throughout the league as a professional, fair-and-square umpire. He worked World Series games, League and Division Championships, and an All-Star game. He called Yankee's Dave Regetti's no-hitter against the Boston Red Sox and in 1978 he worked the one game playoff between the Yankees and Red Sox and was the third base umpire who signaled Bucky Dent's winning home run 'fair'. Palermo's father was a die-hard Sox fan and later admonished his son. "You coulda' saved your mother and me a lot of grief if you'd called it foul." Palermo, who was born in Massachusetts and raised a Red Sox fan, said, "I couldn' Dad, it was twenty feet fair!"

The *Sporting News* ranked Palermo number one among American League umpires in overall performance. Palermo was known to be approachable and when pressed by players or managers about certain calls he made he would explain things in a calm, confident, and composed manner. Catchers in particular liked it when Palermo was behind the plate because he wasn't averse to a little friendly conversation as the game progressed. "Nice curve ball," or, "that was major league heat", he would say enjoying his job.

This attitude served him well in not only in game situations, but later, after the game, at Swannies. And, given the Mariners history of not having a winning record in their first fourteen years of existence, Palermo was usually seated at the bar after another M's loss. Swannie and players knew he was an umpire but never ragged on him for any calls that might have gone against the home team. However, there were a few fans that knew his occupation and if they were drunk enough, they'd question his ancestry. Sometimes under fire at the bar, Palermo employed the same demeanor he demonstrated on the field.

Ironically, Palermo's career was cut short in an incident in 1991 because of his propensity to make the right call. On July 7th, while having dinner with another umpire after a game in Dallas, Palermo was alerted that two of the waitresses from the restaurant were being mugged in the parking lot. He quickly rushed outside to help but was shot in the back by one of the bad guys. Palermo immediately crumbled in a heap, paralyzed from the waist down. The only good news was the assailants were captured. Doctors told Palermo's wife that they doubted that her man would ever walk again.

When Swannie heard about the shooting he sent a letter to his friend at the hospital encouraging him to hang in there and that he would save his seat at the bar. Then Swannie went into action and rounded up a posse that consisted of ballplayers, celebrities, and anybody else that wanted to help put on a benefit night for Palermo.

The benefit was scheduled on a Mariners day off during one of their home stands, and many of the Mariners showed up. Ken Griffey Sr, as well as Ken Griffey Jr served as auctioneers. Edgar Martinez and Tino Martinez (no relation) added star power. The Seahawks' quarterback, Dave Krieg and the Sonics' Gary Payton, were on hand to sign autographs that were later auctioned off.

With Swannie on the mic as Master of ceremonies, the evening was a smashing success. All the celebs on hand signed a huge, 'Get Well Soon' card, which Swannie sent off to Palermo along with a check for several thousand dollars.

The feel-good vibes rolled along through the baseball season (even the Seattle Mariners registered their first ever winning season!). And then, just three months after the shooting, with the aid of a leg brace and a cane, Palermo threw out the ceremonial first pitch in the 91' World Series. He would later say that he drew inspiration to walk again from the many cards and letters he received and gave a special shout-out to the folks at Swannies.

There was one casualty from the night of the benefit however, and it was Swannie himself. During all the hoopla and excitement, he broke his promise to his wife and fell completely off the wagon, resulting in another ride home with his cop pals.

This time when they arrived at his apartment at four in the morning, they announced their arrival with flashing red lights and a quick burst of siren. Many lights in the neighborhood came on, including Swannies'. The cops either thought it was funny, or they were hoping to embarrass their pal enough so that he'd quit drinking again.

When Debbie came out on the balcony to see what was going on, one of the cops yelled up to her, "Everything's okay, Mrs. Swanson, we're just dropping off your husband...again."

This time, instead of thanking the cops, she just shook her head and said, "Keep him." She turned around and went back through the slider door, locking it behind her. Then the light went out in her apartment...and her marriage.

(photo: Rod Long)

Swannie and Dave Henderson at Steve Palermo benefit

CHAPTER FIFTY-NINE

While some couples agree to stay together for the sake of the kids, Debbie wanted to separate for that same reason. She felt her children would be better off in an environment that didn't include so much show biz. The late hours, constant one-liners, jokes, and schmoozing with celebs might be fine for some, but Debbie felt an artificiality to it and wanted to keep her kids from getting too caught up in the whole scene. She wanted her kids to stay grounded. And even though Swannie vowed to change his ways, Debbie knew better. She knew he was wired differently than most. And it wasn't just his drinking, there was something else inside him that needed to be nurtured and fed in order for him to function. He needed to be where the action was. And in a weird way, Debbie thought that maybe it wasn't fair of her to keep him away from his fuel.

So, after a six-month separation, the two settled on the real deal and got a divorce.

Debbie yearned for the values that a small town could offer and wanted to take the kids away from the hustle of Seattle. So, she waited until the kids were out of school for the year and then she moved with Tanner and Lily and Ashley, to Roslyn, Washington, in the Cascade Mountain Range, about eighty miles east of Seattle. Gabriel stayed in the city to live with his father.

The lifestyle change for Debbie and her kids was dramatic. They went from a city with a population of over a half a million people and almost as many cars...to a town of around eight hundred folks and zero traffic lights. Not a one.

Roslyn might seem like a one-horse town to some but it does have its share of history.

It was founded in 1886 as a coal mining town but just six years later suffered the deadliest mine disaster in Washington State history, losing forty-five miners in an explosion and fire. Later that year, a couple of Butch Cassidy cronies robbed the Roslyn bank, thinking that the bank held a huge miner payroll.

They were wrong about the payroll being there, but they did get away with around eight thousand dollars.

Between 1990 and 1995 Roslyn was also the location for filming exterior shots for CBS's hit *Northern Exposure.* Tourists wandering through town today might recognize some of those shots, most notably the Roslyn Cafe camel mural and the store front of the KBHR Radio station.

When Debbie arrived in town, she learned that the film crew for the show was hiring locals for bit parts and extras. She was asked if she or her children might be interested. She politely turned down the offer but when her kids found out about it, they got a little testy.

"Aw, Mom, whaddya doin? We could be on tele*vision*! Everybody would see us. We would be important!"

But Mom stuck to her guns and with a steady hand she set her family's course. "You *are* important. You are the most important things in my life. Always remember that. Now, go finish your homework."

While Debbie was settling in to her new digs, Swannie was doing his best to stay busy. The split from his family may have affected his heart, but not his schedule. In fact, if anything, he may have even upped the pace a little; faster horses, younger women...more whiskey.

Fortunately, Swannie had many good friends that didn't want to see him go completely off the rails. They were there for him and offered their support through his troubling times. One such friend had just gone through a divorce himself and could empathize with the situation. His name was Randy Johnson.

CHAPTER SIXTY

<u>Randy Johnson</u>

Randall David Johnson, born September 10, 1963, was another big-name athlete who could be seen hanging out at Swannies from time to time. Of course, at 6'10", the big left-handed fire-baller could be *seen* just about anywhere he went. H wasn't called the Big Unit for nothing.

Johnson began his big-league career with the Montreal Expo in 1988. He made his debut late in the season on Sept 15, agains the Pittsburgh Pirates, going five innings, striking out five, and earning a 9-4 win. He finished the year with a 2.42 era and posted a 3-0 mark. The future looked bright for Mr. Johnson.

However, the next year he had trouble finding the plate and got off to a horrendous start, going 0-4 in seven games and posting a 6.67 ERA. It was enough to get him traded to the Seattle Mariners on May 25th, 1989.

In his first years with the Mariners, Johnson continued to struggle with his control. He led the league in 'walks issued' three years in a row and rang up an impressive number of hit batsmen. There was no doubt the big man could throw a fastball sometimes clocked over 100 mph, it was just a question of where. Nobody dared dig in at the plate, especially left-handed batters. One such batter was Adam Dunn who said, "The first time you face Johnson you feel like he is going to hit you in the *back* of your neck."

Another left-handed hitter described Johnson's presence o the mound as such; "He was so tall, and his arms were so lon; by the time he finished his delivery he seemed to be close enoug to punch you in the mouth."

But just when you thought he couldn't pitch in the Majors, (twice he walked ten batters in four innings) Johnson would rise to the occasion and throw a gem, like the no-hitter he tossed against Detroit in 1990, or the one-hitter against Oakland in July of '91. To say Johnson was erratic was like saying it sometimes rains in Seattle.

Then one day, Nolan Ryan and the Texas Rangers were in town. Ryan's career was winding down but he had taken an interest in Johnson's situation. He met with Johnson and discussed Johnson's mechanics. Ryan had noticed that Johnson was landing on his heel after delivering the ball, usually causing him to be off kilter in relationship to home plate. Ryan suggested that he should try to land more on the ball of his foot. Johnson took the advice and almost immediately started finding the strike zone.

Later that year, in a game against Ryan and the Rangers, Johnson struck out 18 in 8 innings and threw 160 pitches, a pitch count that will probably never be matched.

Johnson didn't win that game, but the die was cast.

Before his career was over, Johnson would set records and gain awards in the same stratosphere as Nolan Ryan. Among the prizes he notched were five Cy Young Awards, four Warren Spawn Awards, selected to the All Star team ten times, beat every team in the Majors at least once, pitched no hitters in both leagues, threw a perfect game at age forty (oldest to do so) won the pitcher's Triple Crown, which consists of most wins, strikeouts and lowest ERA for the season. He finished his career with 4,875 strikeouts, second only to Nolan Ryan, and most ever for a left-handed pitcher. The list goes on as long as Johnson's arm but you get the idea; Ryan's advice had been money.

You might guess that not everyone was happy with Ryan for passing on his advice. Opposing batters went down with regularity. Tragically, so did a lonesome dove during a spring training game against the San Francisco Giants. It happened in the seventh inning with the Giants' Calvin Murray at the plate and Johnson on the mound. Johnson unleashed a fastball just as the dove entered the 'no-fly-zone' directly in front of home plate. The distance between the pitcher's mound and home plate is 60 feet, six inches, and it's been said that a human brain has .4 second to react to a 90-mph fastball... and that's if he's looking for it! The dove disappeared in a poof of feathers. We assume the dove didn't know what hit him...or her.

Johnson felt bad for killing the bird, and to make matters worse, PETA squawked and thought about bringing charges against him. Later, someone at PETA with a brain bigger than a bird's let Johnson off the hook.

Johnson wasn't particularly fond of the media and could appear annoyed at times during post-game interviews, but later, he liked to mellow out with his teammates and have a beer or two. The fact that Swannies had a reputation for being a safe haven for celebrities, made him feel comfortable there and he could let down his guard a little.

One night after a Mariners game, Swannie and Johnson were at the bar talking about marriage, children, and divorces.

As it neared closing time, Swannie broke off the discussion and went downstairs to his office to wrap things up for the day. As he pulled out a drawer from his desk, he noticed the small container that was about half the size of a lipstick tube. He had forgotten about it but he knew what was in it; cocaine.

It had been given to him by one of the comics as a gift. As mentioned earlier, Swannie wasn't really into drugs, but he wasn't completely innocent either. He decided that a little toot wouldn't hurt, so he tapped out some of the white powder out on the top of his desk, formed a couple of lines with his thumbnail, and rolled up a dollar bill to snort it with. He was halfway through a line when his door suddenly opened and Randy Johnson walked in with a beer in his hand. "Hey, I just remembered something else that might help---" Swannie quickly tried to hide what he was doing, but he was clearly busted.

"Oh, hey Randy, I was just, ah, well...cleaning up here. Ah...*sniff, sniff.* You don't really need to, you know, say anything about this, right?"

Johnson laughed, and walked over to Swannie's desk, wet his finger and gently touched some of the residue that was left on the desktop. He then touched his finger to his tongue for a taste test.

"Hmm." He savored it for a moment like someone sampling a fine wine, and then said, "Okay, my lips are sealed, Swannie. Of course, if you want to pay for my drinks from time to time, that'd be alright too." With that the Big Unit turned and walked out of the door.

Four years later, the Mariners, in their "Why-would-we-ever-want-to-be-in-a-World Series?" wisdom, traded Randy Johnson to the Houston Astros. However, during the years leading up to the trade, The Big Unit was never charged for another drink while he was at Swannies.

CHAPTER SIXTY-ONE

In 1995, after nineteen years of managerial changes, poor draft choices, ownership issues and frustration at about every level, the Seattle Mariners finally made it to the postseason for the first time in franchise history.

Or, another way to look at it; a person could meet someone fall in love, get married, raise a child, send him or her off to college, and be back in time to catch the Mariners in their first ever play-off game.

A generation of losing is certainly a hard pill to swallow for fans and you would think it would matter to ownership as well. In hindsight, the Mariners organization might have been better off hiring Bing Russell to run the ship, at least until they learned out how to win on their own.

But, for the die-hard baseball fans in Seattle, they finally got a taste of how thrilling big-league play-off baseball can be. After advancing from a one-game play-off to determine the American League West Champion, the Mariners were playing at home, tied at two games apiece in a best of five series with the Yankees. The winner of that game would advance and play for the American League Pennant.

And if you couldn't be at the game, the next best place to be was at Swannies. In fact, in might have been even better, given that fans watching at Swannies felt that they had a better kinship with the players than the average fan since they hung at the same bar that the players did. Like brother's, right? You could hear it all the time: "C'mon Edgar. Let's go buddy. Another knock here."

Then: "I know him. He comes in here all the time."

Or: "Yeah, I was in the men's room the other night taking a leak when Buhner walks in, says hi. A regular guy."

Another advantage to being at Swannies rather than *at* the game, you were closer to a bartender. And, boy, was the liquor flowing that day. It was a close game all the way with tensions running high on every pitch. When the game went into extra innings, both teams used one of their regular starters to pitch in relief. Jack McDowell for the Yankees and Randy Johnson for the Mariners.

When the Mariners came from behind to win it in the bottom of the eleventh, Edgar's double scoring Joey Cora from third and Ken Griffey Jr. from first, Swannies and the rest of Seattle went up for grabs.

The instant Griffey slid across home plate with the winning run, every person in Swannies came unglued. Waitresses jumped up on the bar and started dancing. Cooks, bartenders, friends, strangers, cops, teachers, desperadoes, doctors, construction workers, everyone in the joint hugging each other and yelling at the top of their lungs. For a moment Swannie thought that the piano might topple off the wall. Drink orders were shouted.

"Drinks on me! I'm buying!"

"No, I got this, put it on my tab."

It became a drink buying contest with Swannie coming out as the eventual winner. It was a record-setting day at the till.

That night when Swannie finally closed and locked up, he felt a sense of pride. He stood there a moment in a boozy glow and allowed himself to think about how far he had come since borrowing five thousand to open his business. He thought about the people he had met and the things he had accomplished over the years.

But then as he walked away from the door, the sweet smell of success began to give way to melancholy. There was still something missing. Like, maybe a wife and family?

As time went by and his place became even more popular, Swannie began to receive offers to buy him out, offers that he usually ignored, including the one made by his own partner, John Fox.

As the 2001 baseball season rolled along, the Mariners were looking like world beaters, setting records and appearing very much like they were headed to the promise-land. Swannie was so sure of what was to come, he made an off-the-cuff comment to

John Fox that if the Mariners didn't at least win the American League Pennant, he'd sell the bar to him.

And then 9/11 happened and everything stopped.

Later, when it slowly became evident that life would go on, the World Series was played with the Arizona Cardinals beating the New York Yankees in seven games. Ex-Mariner Randy Johnson was named co-MVP of the series.

Like every American, Swannie was deeply moved by the September attacks and went through the stages: shock, disbelief anger, sadness. He thought about how short and fragile life can be and worried about the world his children were growing up in

Thinking about his kids, he vowed to spend more time with them. He also knew that in order to do so, he'd have to make some changes in his life. He would still have to make a living, but maybe he could find a way to do so where he wouldn't be putting in such long hours. With his son's high school graduatio coming up, Swannie made up his mind. His kids were more important than the spotlight. In 2003, he sold his establishment John Fox.

With some of the proceeds from the sale, Swannie bought a restaurant and bowling alley in North Seattle. He let the employees that were already in place run the show and started making regular trips over Snoqualmie Pass to Roslyn. This worked out well for a year or two but after a while Swannie knew there was something else he needed to fix.

So, one day he excused himself from work, went out of town and spent six weeks in rehab. Not long after that, he moved to Roslyn. The Swandog has been sober ever since.

EPILOGUE

When Swannie first asked me to write his story, he asked if he could pay me after the book was finished and on the best seller's list.

My knee-jerk reaction was almost the same as it was the first day he approached me in my car. *Sure, buddy. No problemos.*

But by this time, I had done some research on the Swandog which included watching the documentary, 'Battered Bastards of Baseball', on Netflix, searching through newspaper clippings and Wikipedia-ing every name he threw at me. Calls to former coaches, managers, ballplayers, comics and friends, all confirmed that what Swannie was telling me was true.

In the relatively short time that I've known Swannie it is very hard not to like him. He is a very engaging person and very loyal to you if he likes you. He's a fun guy to be around (most of the time). He's a bit of a con man but because of his personality most people are willing to overlook that part of him.

He asked me how long it would take to write his story and when I gave him my best guess at a year or so he said, "Really? Why so long? I'd like to get it done sooner than that."

I looked at the cigarette in his hand and asked him if he was dying of cancer or something, but he said no, he was just wondering how long these things took.

I was beginning to understand that Swannie could be a little impatient with things. It was part of his DNA. I quickly learned that his mind is always going even if it isn't taking him anywhere.

And then *two* years into this little project, Swannie had a mild stroke that landed him in the hospital overnight. He was released the next day with the suggestion that he take it easy for a couple of days, and for sure, quit smoking. Otherwise he was okay and was cleared to go back to work.

Once he was back on the job we tried to pick up where we left off with his story. He kept saying that there was a lot more he could add to the narrative, about who and what went on at Swannies in the late 90's, but when I asked him what they were, he had difficulty remembering them. It soon became clear that the stroke had muddied his memory. We gave it some time in hopes he could refocus, but after six months with no improvement (and still smoking), we decided to go with what we had.

Now, as we wrap this story up, you can still find Swannie working stand-up comedy at the entry kiosk to the Suncadia resort.

Okay, stand-up comedy is not the real job description, officially he was hired as an information guy at the front gate, but you know, with all those people to talk to when they stop for directions? *And,* it is an eight-hour shift, right? Might as well as some fun, huh?

I'm sure his employer has an idea that how hard it is for Swannie to follow *all* the rules of watch-guy, and perhaps they researched his resume and saw the part about him being Frank Peters' bodyguard, but the visitors and homeowners that drive by his station usually do so smiling. Oh, sure, some folks give him the finger as they pass by, but that's only because they know him.

These days Swannie lives alone in a tiny rented house at the edge of town. Every wall of his bunker is covered with newspaper clippings from the past. Living room, kitchen, bedroom and bath. He has memorabilia scattered everywhere. Baseball bats, gloves, autographed pictures from celebrities and athletes. He even has an autographed picture of Babe Ruth on his wall, although he can't remember how or where he got it. Most of Swannie's life revolves around what used to be. I suppose it's sad in a way but if he chooses to live in the past, at least he has a hell of an exciting past to relive.

Swannie's kids have moved on now with families of their own. His son Tanner is currently a catching coach with the Minnesota Twins and lives twelve hundred miles away with his wife and two children. Daughter Lily lives close by with a daughter of her own. She checks on her Dad from time to time to make sure he's paid his rent and other bills that tend to slip his mind.

When he's not in his greeter's uniform you might find Swannie at the local play-field where he volunteers as umpire for softball tournaments. Or, he might be watching his granddaughter play basketball, or you might find him at the Brick Saloon serving as a judge for the annual running-water spittoon race.

When he's just hanging at the Brick, you can probably catch him around the coffee pot near the main entrance. He's probably nursing a coffee or non-alcoholic beer while he unofficially welcomes everyone that comes in. "Hi, I'm Swannie, only left-handed catcher in baseball. Never made it to the Hall of Fame, but my glove should have. I used to own..."

Or, you might see him driving slowly through town on his way home. His turn signal might be on, probably the left one, but that doesn't mean he's turning. Try not to hold that against him, though; he's a good guy, and he can't remember everything, you know.

Acknowledgments:

A-Team Editors:

Anne Watanabe
Lynn Hatcher

Cover design:

Terry Hamburg, UKC Tribune
Tribune Design Team
terry@nkctribune.com

Contributing editors:

Fiona Gardner, Dan Harden, Dan Williams, Bigal Clasens,
Jimene Smith, Jim Fossett, John and Chris Molvar

Research:

Dr. Butch Woodstrap

and **special thanks to:**

Brad Tacher, GM, KXLE Radio
"Without Brad's help, this project was entirely possible."
(T.C.)

Made in the USA
Las Vegas, NV
11 May 2022

48747234R00132